Francis C. Sessions

In Western Levant

Francis C. Sessions

In Western Levant

ISBN/EAN: 9783337427160

Printed in Europe, USA, Canada, Australia, Japan

Cover: Foto ©Andreas Hilbeck / pixelio.de

More available books at **www.hansebooks.com**

In Western Levant

BY

FRANCIS C. SESSIONS

PRESIDENT OF THE OHIO ARCHÆOLOGICAL AND HISTORICAL SOCIETY

ILLUSTRATED BY

HENRY W. HALL

—..

NEW YORK:

WELCH, FRACKER COMPANY

1890

I am indebted to a friend for the appendix, and for some historical facts which add greatly to the interest of the book.

Francis C. Sessions.

IN GRATEFUL MEMORY

OF MY FRIEND,

DR. J. G. HOLLAND,

WHO ENCOURAGED ME

TO WRITE MY FIRST BOOK.

Madrid

I.

SONETO HEROICO.

*A unas Fiostas de cañas y toros en la plaça de
Valladolid.*

La Plaça un jardin fresco, los tablados
Unencaña do de diversas flores," etc.

Don Louis de Gongora y Argote.

From Madrid Edition, 1654.

A Bull Fight at Valladolid.

Behold! A garden fair, a wide stockade
  Festooned with flowers of every royal hue ;
  Ten roaring bulls like tigers plunging through
The ranks of lancers armed with flashing blade!
Applauding kings, queens, senators, arrayed
  In robes of gorgeous scarlet, gold and blue—
  A wondrous spectacle! Roses and rue
For victor and fallen. Ah, propitious shade
Of Genil and Pisuerga ! here behold
  Our Andalusian gallantries and say
Where now is all your Moorish boast of old ?
  Dead !—vanquished by the glory of this living day.

MADRID.

I.

EVER since reading Washington Irving's "Tales of the Alhambra" and "Conquest of Granada," and Prescott's "History of Ferdinand and Isabella" and "Reign of Philip II.," I have had a great desire to visit Spain, and see for myself the country in which are laid the scenes of the adventures of the sprightly Gil Blas, and of the illustrious knight, Don Quixote.

Very few persons visit Spain in the summer, and I had tried to make ar-

rangements to go in the fall or early
spring ; but failing in that, concluded to
try it in June, and was favored with delightful weather, cool and pleasant.   The
guide-books warn people against traveling in Spain on account of the difficulty
in getting along with the people unless
one can speak the language, the danger
from brigands, and not getting enough
to eat.   Our Spanish guide-book lexicon
seemed to contain just what we did not
want to use, and we had to get along
with what Spanish phrases we could
pick up, and use the sign language for
the remainder.

We enter Spain at Irun, where the
custom-house officer calls on us to open
our baggage for examination.   We had
a hard time to make him understand
that we did not have a trunk.   He gave
up in despair and went away, but returned in a little while with another
passenger.   We had picked up a little
Spanish, so we tried it on him : " *No
tango radoo sujito a derecho*" (I have
nothing liable to duty), but that was
not satisfactory ;   our baggage was
opened and his hands thrust in, but very

gently, and he politely closed it and bid us "*Buenos dias*" (good morning). Here the officers wear a different uniform from the French, and the architecture of the building is different, and the people walk Spanish and talk Spanish, although only a line separates them.

Our next stop was at San Sebastian, and our ride through the Pyrenees and along the Bay of Biscay was quite in contrast with the flat country through which we came from Bordeaux. All around is a grand and picturesque scene of mountain and water. I have rarely looked upon scenery more romantic than that about San Sebastian. It is a most lovely spot on the sea, with mountain and ocean views ; quite a celebrated Spanish summer resort, where the Queen Regent of Spain has a palace. We enjoyed thoroughly our ride into the country, and our visits to the Spanish villages and country people. There are two interesting old cathedrals at San Sebastian—Santa Maria and San Vicente. We go while there to Santa Clara ; a grand scene meets our eyes here. Lomas says of it : " Let real

Spanish sunlight come glinting through
the trees, lie hot on the white horse
shoe of glistening sand that runs around
Santa Clara, light up the blue waves
that dash fiercely even upon ever so still
a day, against the rocks below us, or
the emerald green speck of La Isla, and
make sleepy the old walls of La Monta
that frown out on the world four hundred feet above, and it would be hard to
say what is lacking to make a perfect
picture."

I cannot stop long to talk to you about
Basques, who live on the two slopes of
the Pyrenees ; you see them in San Sebastian, the capital, and other cities in the
north of Spain as they come into market.
There are no villages or large towns in
the Basque provinces ; they occupy the
mountain fastnesses, and their small
houses lie scattered upon nearly all the
heights. You cannot but stop and look
at them in their long breeches, red jackets and sashes, long pointed hempen
shoes and pointed caps ; the women
wear head-dresses of gay colors over
their braided or twisted hair. There is
great equality of conditions and no

nobility, or but few who derive their origin from the time of the Moorish wars. Their language is entirely different from the Spanish or any other known tongue, and they hold on to it with great tenacity. One legend calls it " the language of the angels, with which Adam and Eve used to talk to each other." It is said the devil tried to learn it ; **he** studied it for seven years, but as he then only knew three words, he gave it up. The Andalusians say that in Basque you spell Solomon and pronounce it **Nebuch-adnezzar.**

We must pass on, noticing briefly our visit to old Burgos, the birth-place and the burial-place of the great Spanish warrior of the tenth century, "The Cid." But the greatest attraction here was the grand old Cathedral, Santa Maria la Major, one of the finest Gothic cathedrals in Spain—indeed, in the world. We walked around it and through it, and after going through Burgos we returned again for a careful study of what is, after all, one of the noblest specimens of Gothic structure in the world.

II.

The country between Es Escorial and
the Spanish capital is dreary enough,
and resembles the deserts of sage brush
beyond Nebraska, as you approach Salt
Lake City. Madrid is on a high level
plain, with a gloomy country around it.
As we first viewed it, from a distance, it
looked bright, modern, and Paris-like.
We drove up the hill from the station in
a cab, to which three unruly mules were
attached. The scenes on the street
are truly foreign, and different from
anything we have seen. Our quarters
are at the " Hotel de la Paix," on the
" Puerta del Sol," with a delightful out-
look on a busy, bustling square, with a
great fountain playing, while marching
soldiers and martial music give added
animation to the scene. Everywhere, in
large cities, we see the military, marching by regiments in the streets, with
their short, quick step, quite in contrast
with United States soldiers.

Our Courier, who was a professor, an

educated man, informed us that Spain is now living under the constitution of 1876. Its prominent features are hereditary monarchy in the person and family of Don Alphonso XII, and a legislative assembly of two branches, the Senate and the Congress. The Senate is an aristocratic body composed of three classes.

First.—Senators in their own right, such as sons of the king, grandees of Spain, having a fixed income of 60,000 pesetas ; captains general of the army, admiral of the navy ; the patriarch of the Indies, archbishops, etc.

Second.—A hundred persons nominated by the crown for life.

Third.—One hundred and fifty persons elected by the corporations and the larger taxpayers.

The congress of deputies, founded on general suffrage regulated by the law of elections, consists of persons chosen for five years by electoral districts, in proportion of one deputy to every fifty thousand of the population.

In its general provisions the constitution corresponds in theory to the constitution of other monarchical countries.

There is sufficient flexibility of language under Spanish precedents to allow ample room for the healthy play of parties, and during the twelve years of its existence Spain has had, says Curry, "the conservatism of Canovas and the liberalism of Sagasta and Mont, has survived several military revolts, almost annihilated Carlism, and passed securely over the crisis of a transition from a Bourbon King to the regency of an Austrian woman. In the Cortez there is no longer rule nor previous question. Each speaker can rectify, and with Spanish loquaciousness this system of oratorial ramifications makes debate tedious and an issue remote." Castelar once said, "in the crisis of every party question in Spain the inquiry is, ' What controls the canons?'" The bayonet has superseded the ballot box or a vote of the Cortez. Canovas, the great leader of the conservatives, said that " monarchy is anterior and superior to the constitution." Senor Sagasta, the prime minister, is the leader of the liberal party. The Catholic priests have great influence. At the last election the Jesuits and the monks declared from the pulpit and in the streets that it was a sin against religion and the church to vote for the liberal candidates. Some priests even came to blows with the Liberals. "The conduct of the clergy," says a telegram from Madrid to the London News, "in these elections is sufficient proof that the old spirit of intolerance and the Carlist propensities of the Basque Highlanders are not extinguished." The franchise is now confined, with certain exceptions, to Spaniards who have three conditions; of age, twenty-five years ; of domicile, and five dollars real property tax, or double that amount as industrial tax. Republicans seek to get rid of this last limitation. The registra law is managed so as to keep out as many of the poor as possible. Suffrage is given to all members of academies and ecclesiastical chapters, to all parish priests, and other curates, to all civil servants whose pay is over four hundred dollars a year, to all pensioners (and their number is legion), and to all painters or sculptors who have obtained a first or second class medal. The exceptions have an aristocratic or class ring. The Republicans would place the Roman Catholic and the other churches on the same footing, and proclaim independence of State.

III.

On the streets and everywhere are placards, and boys were selling programmes for the Bull Fight, which was to take place at 4.30 P. M. There were the pictures and names of the bulls and of the performers. Great crowds of well-dressed people, men and women of all classes ; even the Queen and a sister of her husband, the late King Alphonso, were on their way. The conveyances were of all kinds, and such a rush and excitement we have never seen. Men, women and children were all dressed in their best clothes, and looked as if going to an opera. In the boxes were ladies dressed in white, with a white mantilla thrown over their heads, and hanging gracefully down to their feet.

The Bull Fight to-day was one of unusual attraction on account of its being given for the benefit of a city hospital. " A Beneficenca." The usual number of bulls which are brought into the ring at a Bull Fight during the performance is *six*, but at this fight there were to be *eight*. The Plaza de Toros which we entered with from fifteen thousand to twenty thousand *other fools*, is a magnificent building, and must be nearly as large in area as the Colosseum at Rome. It is constructed like the Roman amphitheatre. This has given us an opportunity of seeing the Spanish people in all their crazy enthusiasm in this favorite sport. They would cheer and clap their hands at the least success of the *banderillas* in the hands of the *chulos*, who are men of great activity, avoiding the bulls with skill and thrusting their arrows into them as if educated to their nefarious business. They seem in constant danger of being gored by the irritated and ugly bulls ; sometimes they are killed, but this does not often occur. At a word given by the President a trumpet is sounded and in come the performers on foot and on horses ; the mules, three or

six side by side, harnessed in gay colors,
are there ready to haul out the dead
bulls and horses at the end of each performance, which is done amidst great
cheering. The performers salute the
President, and then comes the bull
through the gate, pawing and rushing
at the men who irritate him by swinging
before him red flags ; he soon approaches
one of the horses, mounted by the man
bull fighter, and then runs away to the
other part of the ring, not caring to gore
him. Then the great audience raised a
terrible howl at his want of courage ;
after being maddened by arrows thrown
into his fore-shoulders, he again, with
head erect and a determined manner,
rushes at the horse and rider, gores the
horse, and raises both horse and rider on
his horns ; the horse falls over with the
rider under him. The fighters rush at
the bull with their red flags to draw him
away ; the horse struggles in the last
throes of death, while the rider is helped
up and led away by two men. The great
crowd cheered and clapped their hands,
and men threw their hats over into the
arena. For a long time the bull was

harrassed and goaded by arrows and poinards and Toledo swords, and after killing four horses, he fell to the ground exhausted, when one of the fighters struck him with a sword and killed him. Then in came the mules with their gay trappings, and with a hurrah from the crowd and music by the band, the bull and the poor dead horses were drawn out. With variations according to circumstances, the same awful fights with like results took place until the last of the eight bulls was killed. When the third bull had killed six horses, it was too much for me, and much to the disgust of our interpreter I left. I was glad to get out into the pure fresh air again and enjoyed a walk in the beautiful parks. On our way to Toledo the next morning, an intelligent Spaniard from Madrid, who could speak English, heard us discussing the horrors of the scenes of the day before, and tried to defend them on account of the early training of the women and children to such scenes as representations of the old Roman arena. I told him that the more slaughter and bloodshed there was the

better the spectators seemed pleased,
and unless a horse was killed there was
no fun in it. The poor horses are the
broken down ones from the cabs and
tramways, and, he said, "they would
have to be killed anyway." The sufferings of the bulls must be intense, but
one's feelings of pity are excited for the
poor horses that are blindfolded and
forced upon the horns of the infuriated
animals, and are sometimes hauled out
of the ring with their intestines trailing
on the ground. To me it was a horrible
scene, and yet it was one which beautiful women and children beheld with
shouts and laughter. When I ask the
guide what all the cheering was for, I
could see nothing, he replied, " The people come here to have a good time, and
a little girl in the gallery waved a flag
which caused the cheering." The Queen
and her sister-in-law used their opera-
glasses continually on the horrible
scenes. I was told to visit the bull fight
as one of the national holiday enter-
tainments, and see for myself ; that one
" might as well see the play of Hamlet
with Hamlet left out as to go to Spain

and not see the national entertainment."
It was a remarkable experience ; the
throngs of eager, excited people all
making their way to one place, stirred
as nought but the prospect of bloodshed
can stir them ; the swaying of the ever
increasing mass around the walls and
barriers of the grim looking charnel-
house ; and then to stand and look down
upon the seething crowd of some twenty
thousand souls around and beneath, all
absorbed in the one desire, from the
elegantly dressed dames and cavaliers of
the upper tiers, (where we were) down
the sloping rows of crowded benches
below us.

I brought to the hotel with me a daily
paper with three column slang of the
bull fight, and asked our courier to
translate it ; he replied "it is impossible, as it is written in the customary
slang of the arena and the editor manu-
factures highfalutin words for the occasion."

This national *fiesta*—disgusting, de-
moralizing, cruel, bloody—is probably
the most distinctive characteristic of
Spain. Our traveling companion to To-

ledo, who was a native of Madrid, said that some of the better classes, had tried to legislate against it, but the opposition it provoked was violent and revolutionary.

---

* See Appendix, note I, on the antiquity of bull-fighting and bull-baiting.

II.

The Beauty of the Madrillian Women. As to the peculiar beauty and interest of Spanish women, the volumes that are filled with amenities and panegyric, leave volumes yet to be written, and even then the tale but half told. Everywhere there are types—distinct, contrasting, definitive. Moorish sagacity, Roman resoluteness, Oriental depth of eyes or mediæval sensuousness, each distinct and dramatic upon the passing faces, makes the market-places and avenues of

Madrid appear to be a sort of symposium, to which are invited, not only the representatives of a living present, but the purest types of the past. The dark, sparkling eyes, rich jet black hair, graceful litheness of figure and movement, and above all, that undefinable art which so successfully conceals the consciousness of its own grace and beauty —all these combine to make the Spanish woman an admirable exponent of the science of pleasing, and a peculiarly interesting study to the thoughtful foreigner. The children and young maidens are particularly strong in the native characteristics, as are the aged, who have sunk back into elegant repose after a life of conventional hurry and tumult. Study the children and the aged, if you would know a nation's ruling character. The former have not yet learned, and the latter have long since discarded, the foreign innuendoes which their contact with northern races has imparted them, and which affectation so ill becomes the conservative dignity of the true southern type. Then, too, before the battle of life has buried the native character in a sort of cuirass of conventionality, and after this useless assumption for the benefit of trade and social policy is laid aside, the quality which in middle life is impenetrable, in childhood and old age lies upon the surface But commerce the great revolutionizer of nations, the destroyer of the conservative and the old, and the god-father of the progressive the superficial and the new, is fast making inroads into the Spanish character, the displaced southern nature yielding to a northern principle (admirable in its place, but most ignoble out of it), and, like that of Japan, the national character will become assimilated with foreign substance till all distinguishing types sink to blend in a sort of universal composite and unvarying whole Commerce takes the ends of a thousand threads, from as many peoples, and of the great dissimilar many-colored mass each differing from the other in quality, virtue, and principle, weaves a solid, grey, neutral fabric, which, though it clothes well the universal, leaves naked the individual. This seems to be the

compensation of nature. We thank commerce for uplifting the mass, while we
ever recognize that it is a bounty which
crushes all types. The unit becomes
complex ; the individual, composite; the
accidental, the characteristic and the
extraneous become the analogous, the
uniform and the monotonous. In this
spirit comes the sense of regret at the
fall of the *mantilla* or veil, which has
graced the dark-haired Spanish head for
so many centuries, and about which float
so many delightful legends and the airs
of lost arts, and which is fast being
discarded in favor of the less becoming
importations from France. Notwithstanding, the women of the older, more
conservative of the Madrillians still retain the happy ornament, and revive in
the heart the memory of Roderigo, the
Enchanted Armor, and the perils and
amenities of Gil Blas of Santillana.
There is a period between childhood and
womanhood, however, when the young
maiden is kept under strictest surveil-
lance The Sancho Panza proverb has
it, and rather dryly. it is true : " *Que la
Doucella honrada, la pierna quebrada y en*

casa," "the virtuous maiden and the broken leg must both stay at home." But though the study of this captive period of the Spanish woman's life is denied the unacquainted foreigner, the rest is delightfully interesting to one traveling from the North. From the lands of intense activities, dead, soulless, though sturdy, honest faces that seldom beam as if the great blazing sun were reflected in them, it is truly a feast to observe the Southern female character, with its rich bequests of subtle distinction and qualities of repose from the East, the eyes like the calm, steady flame of an altar lamp, passionate mouth, and soft Southern complexion, and recall the dignity of a great past, which remains now but by tokens and hints, and which will soon disappear forever.

In and About the City of Madrid. We presented our letter from Senator Sherman to ex-Senator Palmer, of Michigan, now our national representative to Spain. We were received most cordially, and were afterwards presented to the minister's secretary, Captain Hamilton, of the

United States Army, who is an Ohioan. The minister was received very graciously yesterday by the Queen Regent Christiana, at her palace. Her address of welcome, and the happy reply of our minister, show the kind feeling that exists between Spain and the United States. The generous ex-Senator gave me a letter to the honorable *President del Congresso de las Cortez,* Don Manuel Alonzo Martinez, asking him to grant us admission to the exciting debate which was to take place that afternoon. We were delightfully entertained, and notwithstanding the fact that great crowds of the *élite* of Madrid were unable to gain admission to hear the debate, we were escorted to the President's gallery. The plainness and narrowness of the congressional chamber rather surprised me. The hall is not as roomy as our Superior Court chamber in the Capitol at Washington, the seats are common cane settees, and the conspicuous absence of the desk, that one thing essential to our Congressman's authority, was one of the first objects of remark. The Senate, or rather, the Congress, is composed of two hundred and fifty members, and a fine body of men they appear to the stranger. Most of the members are young, and all are vigorous, able and strikingly military in their dignified bearing. Doubtless there was an additional degree of frictional heat firing the honorable body that day, for the majority, which is the liberal party, was being violently attacked by the conservatives, an occasion of great excitement in the Spanish capitol. Castellar, the great liberal leader and orator, was present, but, to our disappointment, he remained silent. He is a man short in stature, with a large, fine forehead, strong features that indicate the impressible Spanish type, and a bearing of splendid dignity, giving one the impression of great mental and physical power.

Madrid itself is a most attractive city, but our Spanish traveling companion to Toledo informed me that the ratio of mortality is higher than that of any other city of Europe, a fact that surprised me. It is doubtless on account of the cold winds which sweep across the

plains from the snow on the Appenines,
which we see all the way from San Sebastian.   Certainly the worst atrocity
ever committed by Philip the Second,
who was styled by Jovellanos " El
Escurialense," after that gloomy monument to his own fanatical and incon-
stant career, was when he chose Madrid
as the great Spanish metropolis.   The
water is very brackish, like that of the
alkali country of Nebraska, and the
dreary plains about it remind one of
those western sage-brush deserts around
Great Salt Lake.   Spain abounds in
splendid sites, accessible to navigation,
interesting in picturesqueness, and noble
possibilities ; and why this uninteresting
spot should have been chosen, can only
be accounted for by taking due account
of the influence of Philip's mad grandmother, "Crazy Jane," upon that unfortunate despot, proudest of kings and
devoutest of monks.   Everything is exotic in this city, which stands as a swarn-
ing oasis on a desert of low brush, which
ought to be fertile, thus cheapening the
products which now are brought from
great   distances.   Mule   trains   from

Asturias, some thirty miles, bring but-
ter ; from Aranjuez, equally far distant,
apricots, lemons and dates ; from Aragon
and Toledo, further still, vegetables and
olives. Every part of Spain pours into
this great hole in the center of a wilderness its choicest and chiefest products.
So the proverb that *" Pagan d las veces
justos por pecadores,"* " the righteous often
pay for the follies of sinners," becomes
illustrated with vehemence when we
behold the generations paying precious
tribute to the stupidity of this ignobly
dead and magnificently buried Philip.

Velasquez and Mu-   P r o b a b l y the most
rillo.   noteworthy object of interest in Madrid to the foreigner is the
Royal Art Gallery, which is said to contain more first-class works of the old
masters than any other gallery in Europe. I was particularly interested in
those representations of Velasquez and
Murillo, the former excelling in his portraits, the latter in his mixing familiar
nature with the most exalted objects—
the idealization of the commonplace, the

etherealizing of fact. As for Velasquez,
it was my astonishment that such a
flattered and favored courtier of the
fourth Phillip could do any serious work
at all ; or, on the other hand, that such
a versatile and laborious artist could
have had any time to court and be
courted. But whatever that tremendous
mind undertook, it was performed *a
facile princeps*, with a grace that conceals its toilsomè and elaborate pains-
taking. I doubt not that in Europe no
works can be found which so admirably
illustrate at once the impressibility and
the individuality of genius. He saw a
Rubens, the equestrian St. George, and
immediately painted Philip the Third.
He saw a Rizi, bearing all the intricacies
of the chiaro-scuro, and immediately
painted the Austrian portraits, the imi-
tator always equal, and often superior,
to his prototype.*

---

* See Appendix, Note II, Anecdotes of Velasquez and
Murillo.

Toledo

II.

"The idle forge that formed Toledo's blade."—*Byron*.

"A most sweet Spaniard—a confit-maker of Toledo—
that can teach sugar to slip down your throat a
million of ways."—*Sun's Darling*.

TOLEDO.

I.

.

The Regal City. It is with great interest that we approach the famous old city of Toledo, once an empire within itself ; king, throne and realm, and with a weird, glowing history that filled volumes, while contemporary England's would scarcely fill a chapter. What a wonderful reliquary to attest the reign of the Roman dethronement of the Jew ; the Goth dethronement by the Roman ; the Moor, by the Goth ; and at last, with but the shreds and patches of a departed glory, the catholic Spaniard

in the ascendency.   Each conqueror and
his followers left an imperishable history, and a living landmark at every
hand.

The city seems to have been built
upon the most sightly and imposing
eminence in Spain, and is in striking
contrast with Madrid in this particular.
As we approach the city the sun
brightens all the sharp pinnacles against
the southern blue sky with almost a
fierce glamor ; but later in the day, the
hard lights soften and grow almost
melancholy in the dull harmony of the
tints and the shadows close about the
city from beneath, till at last to an observer from a distance, the great " Imperial Metropolis " seems to hang in
mid-air, like the coffin of the Mahommet
whose followers left such irradicable
traces upon it.   The city is like a magnificent sepulchre, silent as the chambers
of the pyramids, and with its labyrinthine streets, so narrow that oftentimes
one must turn sidewise to pass a traveler, is like a monastery of some strange
sect, the last of whose adherents has
fallen.

We were driven across the bridge over the Tagus through the ascending, narrow thoroughfares to our hotel, which we found one of the most interesting old interiors in Spain. In Moorish times it was a palace of a dignitary under the sovereign, with inner court and ancient surroundings and stone stables for the keeping of the Andalusian steeds. The gates of the city, together with the great walls that rib the brow of the hill, are highly picturesque in their semi-dilapidation, the *Puerta del Sol* and the *Puerta de Visagra*, both of the purest Saracenic architecture. Like the old buildings, they are dignified and imposing.

Upon our emerging into the narrow streets, and following the labyrinthine ways, which led through the most luxuriant of ancient courts, and by the most dilapidated architectural relics, we are carried back in imagination a thousand years. The ancient doors, studded with huge nails, and the relics of ancient and unique design, the wide courts with crennelated walls and blooming ivies, —everything decorative bearing such an

individual stamp in design and workmanship, that the student of antiquity
and comparative history finds himself
here in his veriest element. " Few cities
that I have seen," says Street, " can
compete in architectural interest with
Toledo, and none perhaps come up to it
in the singular magnificence of its situa-
tion, and the endless novelty and picturesqueness of its every corner. It
epitomizes the whole strange history of
Spain in a manner so vivid, that he who
visits its odd nooks and corners carefully
and thoughtfully, can work out almost
unassisted the strange variety which
that history affords."

II.

The Hospital. Our courier called our
attention to the old
foundling hospital of Santa Cruz, which
he said was endowed by Cardinal Men-
doza, who died in 1495. Its establish-
ment was under the direction of Queen
Isabella. Historians say that the Cardinal ought to have given largely for

such a hospital, to atone for certain youthful indiscretions laid to his charge. Such an institution was needed in Spain at that time, judging from history.

III.

The Beggars. The beggars in the streets were so numerous and so persistent that we could scarcely make our way along. Most of them are children trained to the profession, a most lamentable fact. Many of the older beggars would exhibit themselves with an arm or leg missing. Our guide caught one of these, and to our dismay, we found that he had a clever way of tying up the leg to appear as if he had lost it. All through Spain the beggars are more numerous than in any part of the world we have visited. In Madrid, girls from eight to twelve years of age clamor after the stranger, importuning him almost viciously ; and if one declines to give them anything, or attempts to drive them away, they shower upon him the vilest of invectives. Our guide reported the remarks of one of these pert Arabs of the street who said, " Go on, you are not a man ; you are half man and half woman," followed by an oath.

IV.

The Transito, etc.   There are so many buildings of such great interest here that I can only mention a few, and will not undertake to give particular description of any.   One was the Transito, a synagogue, built in the beginning of the fourteenth century by Samuel Levi ; also another synagogue, called Santa Maria La Blanca, built in the middle of the eleventh century by Israel David Forache.   The imposing church of San Juan de los Reyes was built under the catholic regime of Ferdinand and Isabella, after the surrender of Granada.   The cloister of this church is carved and ornamented in the purest Gothic style.

We visited the old manufactory of cutlery, where the famous Toledo blades are still made.   We bought a small sword and a pair of scissors with the

Toledo brand upon them. The work-
men no longer possess the skill in this
department, however, which their pre-
decessors exclusively enjoyed.

V.

Feminine Beauty. To the student of the
beautiful and true, in all
these multiplied phases in nature human
and material, the feminine face is the
richest, and most joy-giving of all the
varied texts for his reflections and senti-
ment. And nowhere, it seems to me,
does the nature simple, and withal,
austere in its earnestness, come so close
to the surface as in the clear, limpid
countenance of the Spanish woman,
who wears the reflections of her best
qualities in the luminous depth of her
very eyes, in the warm, sunny innocence
of her smiles, and on the cheek that
changes like the sensitive plant, giving
emphasis to every passion or uncertainty
of the heart, every perturbation of the
mind. And it is marvelous how a few
drops of foreign blood mixed with the
clear quality of the ancestral nature will

change the whole temperament, giving
it an added grace oftentimes, but generally, like the grafting of trees, where the
limb of the coarser northern fruit is
grafted upon the finer trunk, it is rather
to the bane of the issue than to its refin-
ing. The development of the human
species is, after all, like that of the peach.
Either by the most scientific or for-
tuitous principles these very Arabs
evolved the fine grained, downy-coated
fruit of exquisite fibre—the real gentility
of horticulture—from material of a
grosser nature. The Andalusians are
expressly the most refined. In a
country like this, where the provinces
bear from each other that distinctive
quality which impresses the traveler
passing from place to place with the
fact that he has passed the frontier and
is never allowed to forget it, certain
provinces are prone to cultivate charms
which, in the province adjoining, is dis-
regarded ; or, if not that, at least unde-
veloped in the zeal of perfecting one of
its own peculiar attractions. For instance, in the north of Spain, can be
found the most perfect figures and the

most faultless hands and feet ; in Seville, by far the most graceful manners ;
in Madrid, the most engaging facial expressions, sensitive to every light and
shade of thought and mood, while in the
south the women are adorned with
the most perfect teeth and hair. But if
the development of a painter was entrusted to the most knowing collaborator
with nature, he would rear his fine-heart-
ed Murillo in Seville, just as by good fortune or by the external fitness of things,
was the case. Murillo could not have
found nobler types nor more perfect sym-
metry of feature than in the very streets
of the place of his birth and maturity.
Painter of Madonnas and beggars with
equal superiority of touch, he had not to
go beyond his own doorstep to study his
theme. The times were ripe, the country
was fruitful, the church with its zeal-
ous spirituality in highest authority,
and Philip a patron of arts. And now the
traces, not altogether dimmed, of the
womanly and manly nature which Murillo so etherealized, remains as a divine link between the purity of the past
and the joy of the present.

VI.

The Spirit of the Place. H o w thoroughly in keeping with the Spanish spirit is everything met in this city of departed splendor! The old palaces, grim and spectral, like great skulls untenanted, with mouths that grin, and eyeless fronts down which a long black wrinkle zig-zags as if a flash of lightning had struck it ; the leaning towers —not purposely aslant as in Italy, but made so by the slow change of the earth's formation—the great gates that lead into interminable depths that know no footsteps, and vaulting arches that beckon one into what was once the guarded bowers of the Moslem nobles, now overgrown with wild geranium, iris and poppy, which struggle so hard to keep up the ancient autocracy of romance and beauty. But what seizes the mind more than anything in Toledo, is the unutterable sense of isolation—the solitude, the estrangement, the awful serenity of the sacred historical spot.

What a refuge is this from the clamors of cosmopolitan Europe—for this seems not a part of the continent, indeed— what a place to possess one's self of the true spirit of Mohammedan days, shut out alike from all the consolatory faces of friends and the ignoring of the commonplace! Here is the rare spot where it is possible to be alone yet befriended most confidently; to be "solitary, yet not desolate; a unit in aggregate."

The fragmentary statue, the dust-laden portrait, the crumbling inscription which gives one just a happy glimpse into some Eleusian mystery, that leaves to the weaving of the imagination the rest of the solid fabric— all these are company, and what great company, indeed! "Silence, her sacred self, is multiplied and rendered more intense by sympathy." The very pavements that seem to yield beneath one's tread, the very moss-grown thresholds hollowed down by the soft sandal of the Moorish maiden and the burly *matador*, the glimpses across the chasm of the Tagus, which but reveals another picture of impressive solitude—all con-

spire to give point and zest to the happy
turn of Richard Fleckno's apostrophe :

" Stillborn silence ! thou that art
Flood-gate of the deeper heart ! "

VII.

The Castle.

The Alcazar stands on
an eminence above the
chasm of the Tagus like a solitary sentinel. The portals, venerable and tot-
tering, but for all their age, the most
commanding of our respect, leads us into
a wide court, as in all oriental palaces.
Here and there stand grim torsos, and
unpedestaled effigies of kings unnamed,
unsung by the present generation of
vipers who sleep, sleep, sleep the live-
long day in the shady nooks, between
the cool walls and under the ruined
porticoes, heedless even of a foreign
footstep. The ban of the old Alcazar is
lifted ! Let who will cross the threshold, he will be unmolested, unnoticed.
No sly eunuch stands guarding the marble lattice ; no scimetar, like the sword
of Damocles, hangs over the head of the
giaour for venturing upon the threshold
of the chamber of the beautiful Florinda.
He may enter where he will, surprised

here and there by a lazy beggar, or a
still more lazy workman, who pretends
to be restoring—alas ! this pretending to
pretensions—but neither the shade of
Roderick, nor of Count Julian, whom
his king so wronged, nor Alonzo, nor
Charles, nor Philip—not even Napoleon,
will interdict him.

The grim Alcazar is a splendid setting
to so fervent and exalted a piece of history. Certainly the chronicles of no
European country rivals it in interest.
What hand can take up the pen in por-
trayal of such magical, phantasmic
dramas of war and peace which have so
sturdy a foundation in fact, without
more or less unconsciously imbuing the
subject with a spirit that finds in legend
and tradition with all their crowding
ranks of warriors and fair women, such
hearty champions ! So full of poetry,
pathos, and that distinct coloring of the
times so easy to feel, so difficult to de-
scribe, is the story of Don Roderick,
king of the Goths, and the beautiful
Moorish captive, Elyata, who, cast upon
the southern shores while on her be-
trothel voyage to Tunis, was sent in

great state as a favored prisoner to the king, and after remaining a long time in her magnificent captivity, changed her faith, and became the queen of all the Gothic realm. Then follows the story of Roderick's favorite courtier, Count Julian, who, "as unto a brother," entrusts his beautiful daughter to the guardianship and protection of his king, while he himself goes to the Straits to protect the country from Moslem invasion. Then comes the betrayal of the beautiful woman, even under the royal roof, to the dishonor of the entrusted king himself ; and that piteous wail from the innocent heart, penned in blood and tear-drops, which reaches the father who so loved and confided in his lord, whereupon, bent upon revenge, he allies himself with the Arabs, and the land of the Goths is changed to the "Imperial Paradise of the Faithful to Allah !" Then begins that marvelous civilization, which is destined to throw Christian Europe into an eclipse, from which, belittling, barbaric twilight, it rallies only after the struggle of centuries.

VIII.

In this area of struggle *Repose.* **for a certain happiness,** which may be said to be artificial at best, when nations repose in the guarded vigilance of their neighbors, feeling security only in that peace which never forgets the imminence of war, and placing confidence only in the compact with that neighbor whose military resources are less than theirs, to estrange one's self from this invidious secret tyranny of modern life, and find real repose and happiness in the contemplation of such classic and noble reliquaries as are here before us in the historical arcades and courts of Toledo, certainly gives weight and argument to the daring conviction of Emerson—that "life is an ecstasy." And who, rather than an American, can take deep pleasure in such contemplations, since of all others he is a creature of the new, the progressive, the future? We Americans live in the present, using the past only as incidents of precedence, to avoid errors and correct the evils which have been preserved to us ; but having so comparatively little history, we cannot realize the true spirit of worship which clings about old ruins and long-time usages. We have a respect but for the material purposes in life. Yet, face to face with so splendid a relic of a splendid age of civilization, this oasis of culture and learning in the great dark desert of mediæval Europe, who better than an American can understand the spirit which prompts this history-worship in others ? We stand outside the circle, as it were, on an eminence looking into valleys whose magic tints and harmonies we enjoy as a whole, but we never can descend and become one of the people wh ɔ live, move, and have their being therein. The position of a thoughtful American abroad is a peculiar one, and one of true privilege. Unhampered by ancient prejudices, unbiased by the severe patriotism of jealous nations, never warped in judgment by hard training in a single partisan hatred, nor suffering his opinions to receive color from the solecisms of monarchial and hierarchial forms and pre-

cedents, he surveys the whole field with
the eye of a true reasoner. And here in
the heart of Spain, of all countries the
most highly luminous by the magic
lights of history and romance, the heart
is enchanted out of its dull prosaic
world, and given privilege to revel at
will in the superb fictions and realities
of a departed glory. The very climate
of Spain is conducive to contemplation
and thoughts. The repose is so perfect, the cities so full of sunshine
and shadow in contrasting extremes,
and the people everywhere seemingly so
original and creative. Fact has gathered
about it such a tinge of fancy, and sweet
illusions have taken upon themselves
such colors of reality, that he is a wise
discriminator who knows the line where
the myth ends and the stern actuality
begins. Everywhere does history, ever
superior to fiction, outdo even its own
forerunner, and make fact more fanci-
fully enchanting than legend.

IX.

The Saracens. What a wonderful country and period of civilization was that which followed the successful conquests of Tarik and the Emir Musa, and how vastly in contrast with the barbarity of the Christian countries contemporary with the Saracenic rulers ! On one side, Italy, the picture of abject squalor and degradation into which the ignorant shrine-worshippers had fallen ; above them, the strifes of Charlemagne and Pope Hadrian against all the opposing principalities, and within the enchanted provinces a contrasting picture of art and culture that awes the student of comparative history, and leads him to discredit the evidences were they not so luminously verified by these magnificent reliquaries at each hand. And now, wandering through the huge arcades and splendid courts, watching the clear southern sunbeams falling athwart the marble arches and lighting up the mosaics and iridescent abrabesques as

with a fond benediction, it does not seem
that so many centuries of change and
tribulation have intervened ; but that
momently there must appear through
the fairy vistas of alabaster and marble,
the fair faces of the court favorites—the
beautiful Zaras, Zaidas and Zelindas, of
the great Emir—and then follow the
low, whispering murmur of lutes, the
song of the dancing girl before the sul-
tana, the soft, gliding hiss of the eunuch's slipper on the ccol mosaics, and
the tinkling treble of the fountains of
quicksilver beyond.   From these variegated archives to wander forth into the
surrounding gardens, it really seems
that the white bournouses of the Faithful
must still lie prostrate on the flagging,
offering up their prayers and thanks for
this the paradise promised of the exalted
Koran ; and that we must meet ever
and anon, pacing up and down the
shady retreats, amid the bowers and
hanging gardens, the wise Averroes, the
philosopher, resolving in his mind the
solution of his theory of the unity of
souls though parted among millions of
individuals ; or Avenzoar, the Nestor of

chemistry, discovering laws and sciences for which we ourselves are indebted to him, as the Arab words invented by him —in common use to-day, such as alcohol, syrup, elixir, and countless others —will attest. Everything that the Arabs in their splendid civilization touched, they beautified, enlarged and perfected. Ben Musa, with the geometry of the Ptolemies, deduces a system which he names Algebra. Almaimon, while the Inquisition at Rome threatened death to any who disputed the fact that the earth was flat, visits all the foremost philosophers of the East, and on the shores of the Red Sea, measures a degree and determines within a few miles the circumference of the earth. Sufi corrects the errors in the photometry of the stars. Alhazen discovers the law of terrestrial gravitation ; solves the great optical problem proving that, contrary to the Greek and Egyptian scientists, rays of light do not issue forth from the eye, but from external objects pass into it ; and, more wonderful still, proves the curvilinear path of sunlight by which the apparent illusion that we see the

sun long before it rises and long after it
sets, is made an indisputable fact.   How
marvelous is all this !   How little do we
realize what we owe to these splendid
usurpers, who, by long residence and
magnificent achievements, made this
land a garden of beauty, a seat of learning, a school of civilization for the whole
world.   If you would know what the
Arabs in Spain have done for us, attempt by Roman notation to multiply
the days of the year by an equal number, and see what an almost limitless
task it is.   They invented the cannon,
and if they did not invent, they certainly
were the first to effectively use gun-
powder.   They introduced silk and cot-
ton from the   East, and perfected its
weaving, while half of Christian Europe
were clothing themselves in skins and
straw-coats.   Among their achievements
are the   Toledo   blades, the Morocco
leather—the secret of which, when they
were expelled, they took to Morocco,
whence the name—the plants of the domestic garden, the peach, the plum and
the perfection of the apple ; the intro-
duction of the mariner's compass, rice

and sugar from the East, and the perfection of the latter's processes of manu-
facture. Miles of street lamps, when
Rome and Paris were benighted, graced
their cities ; pavements, when the Pope
stepped from the Vatican into the mud ;
hot and cold baths, when Christian
Europe wallowed in squalor ; perfumed
halls of magnificient proportions, while
Christian Europe lived in huts and huge
stone castles unfit for stables. The
Andalusian horses—the noblest breed
that lends such a grace of chivalry to
the times—the art which found in
arabesques an opportunity to display
the genius that the Koran denied in the
pictorial art : all of these wonderful evidences of that noble civilization cannot
be ignored, and when face to face with
these marvels of architecture and
science, become the more convincingly
real.

But farewell, Toledo ! grave, venerable and full of sorrow—"thou that
listenest to the sighs of orphans, and
drinkest the tears of children, at length
I am dismissed from thee. The time is
come at last that I no more should pace

thy never-ending terraces," as the eloquent De Quincy makes worthy note,
"no more to dream," and wake thence
into the captivity of the present with its
rule of the common place.   Adieu to
thy blackened streets, narrow and hol-
low-sounding as a sepulchre ; to thy
courts, reverbrating in solitude the
voice of eternity ; to thy empire of beggars, who, by the splendid dignity of
their profession and faith, and in the religious divinity of beggar-lineage blest
them from father to son since the time of
Philip—that beggar most of sovereigns,
even in purple robes—make it an honor
for a foreign barbarian like me to toss
them a goodly handful of coppers.

So we pass the threshold of the great
gloom-city, the blackened portals yawn-
ing like a toothless old centurion ; cross
the great stone bridge which threads the
chasm of the Tagus, the depressing silence and gloom of the mammoth old
piles growing more penetrating with
the lifting of the damp mists from the
ravine where "flows fast by the oracle"
the rushing waters which have run red
from the hearts of nations into the great

chalice of history. Everywhere the
cold, sullen tints of the earth and the
rocks that prop the fortress, along the
verge of the cold abyss which sends up
the white vapors as an incense of
irony, the sombre tints of the west
where the sun leaves but a ragged line
like a flash of fire, intensify the reverence which so profound a historian inspires. Then dies even the sound of the
waters, and fades the higher lights along
the low verge of the fortress, and one
by one the pinnacles and towers merge
into the melancholy distance, and we at
last realize the force of the touch of an-
guish in that poet of Andalusian memories, when he speaks as from a broken
heart—

> " Negra, ruinosa, sola y olvidada
> hundidos ya los pies entre la arena
> alli yace Toledo abandonada,
> azotada del viento y del turbion !"
>
> ZORRILLA.

> In gloom, forsaken, sorrowing alone,
>   Now do my footsteps falter in the sands,
>   Where like a naked child Toledo stands,
> Lashed by the tempest answering moan with moan :

See Note III. Appendix.

Cordova

IV.

" Gold not so pure, nor pearls so fair,
  As God hath made thee, child divine !
No mines of Ind or Afric rare
  Hold gems that match this look of thine.

" To Allah praise that of the earth
  No thing more beautiful can be
Than maiden grace and woman's worth,
  United Godwise as in thee."
  *From the Arabic of Abdallah Xamri, poet to
the Court of Abderahman.*

" Oh, royalty ! what joys hast thou to boast to recom-
pense thy cares ? "—*Dowe's Sethona.*

CORDOVA.

I.

On to Cordova, "The Beautiful." We had for our companions on the night-ride to Cordova a Spanish family, represented by an aged grandmother, the grandson and children, whose charming native manners and mutual tokens of respect much pleased and charmed us. In parting at the depot there were great demonstrations of regret, with gesticulations and osculations enough to warrant the seriousness of a trip through to eternity. Provisions and wine in great

abundance were their happy accom-
paniments, and four times during the
night the huge hampers were attacked
with vigor and certain success, not even
forgetting the good old lady of eighty
who gave the several feastings a gravity
of which none lost sight for a moment.
They were exceedingly polite to us, and
asked us to partake with them. The
Spanish have the custom of saying to a
stranger, "I make you a present of my
home!" if you are to be their guest;
but it is not necessary to state, this
generosity is given with certain clauses
of modification. Their pert chattering
reminded us of a flock of English spar-
rows on a June morning. The Spaniards seem to me to be even more polite
than the French. All expect courtesy
from you, and are too well bred to
notice the slight if by some little inad-
vertence they do not receive it.

Our hotel at Cordova was the Fonda
Suiza, which can boast of a pleasant
patio, or court, paved with marble, and
a stairway of marble quite as imposing
as any we have seen. At each landing
there is a different pattern of mosaic.

All the inns of Andalusia have gardens of flowers, fountains and trees, to
adorn the old palaces of the departed
conservative aristocracy, which are now
changed into hospices for the entertainment of strangers.

II.

The streets of Cordova
About the City.   are so narrow and labyrinthine that without a guide it would
be quite impossible to make one's way
about.   One of the first objects of our
seeking was, of course, the old Mosque,
about which we have read so often,
passing on the way several palaces and
private hotels, through the open gate-
ways of which we enjoyed glimpses of
the beautiful gardens and luxuriant
courts which, so attractive to the an-
cients, seem to be no less so to those
who have kept them unfading in beauty, with but the dignity of age and
antiquity to ripen and mellow the contrasting tints.   One ancient Roman
gateway in particular, led us through
an open court and down a narrow path

through a grove of old orange trees, which we were told were three hundred years old. The tops of these venerable trees were blighted by the cold and snow of last winter, a parallel of which, in severity, had never been known before by the oldest inhabitants. The old Mosque, which was the particular object of our walk, almost bewildered us by the infinite number of columns of different colored marble, and the variety of the carved work around them. This marble was brought from Jerusalem, Morocco, Algeria, Alexandria, and many other contiguous countries. The pillars, as has often been said, resemble a forest. Though formerly they were twelve hundred, there are now only eight hundred in number, that look which way you will, seem to stand in rows. Various designs, worked upon some of them by prisoners with their finger nails, were almost as fantastic as the legend which would convince us of their truth.

III.

The Mihrab. The Mihrab, or sanctuary of the Mosque, was worthy of especial consideration; the marble floor was worn round the outer edge by the Moslems walking about it on their knees as a part of their worship. Unfortunately for the artistic *ensemble*, Charles V. had a choir erected in the center, thereby destroying the beauty and harmony of the interior. What a splendid sight it must have been, the weird Moorish architecture, lighted up with thousands of gold and silver lamps ! The mosque has been so changed by vandals that one can only get a glimpse of its old splendor. Great preparations were being made in the mosque for the *Corpus Christi* holiday which occurs on the first Thursday after Trinity Sunday. The great organ was being played by a monk, the most famous organist in Spain, and the voices of the monkish choir, blending the music of the organ, reverbrated through the great mosque sometimes like the roar of distant thunder,

then as soft and sweet as a flute. As I
walked around those great halls, I tried
to picture to myself the pristine glory
and splendid achievements of the Moors,
almost wishing that they had never been
driven from their paradise. Although
Moslems are worshippers by the scriptures of the Koran, if they had lived and
gone on in their wonderful achievements,
would not Spain have been a much
greater and renowned nation than to-
day, with its bull-fights and priestly
domination ? In this grand. old mosque
are found the Roman, Moorish and
Gothic styles of architecture. The treas-
ury in this church, containing many gold
relics and precious stones, was robbed in
1870, and it is now constantly guarded
by six sentinels of the cathedral of Cordova, who each hold a separate key to a
separate lock. By permission of the
Archbishop, we entered with three canons of the church, who had come from a
distance, to see the treasures. One of
the relics was a *Corpus Christi* gold temple about ten feet high and three feet
at the base, with a statue of the Messiah
in the center, built, in 1494, of the pre-

cious ore brought by Columbus from the newly-discovered America. One arch-bishop and one hundred canons are de-pendencies of this celebrated mosque, now changed into a Catholic cathedral. Our companions said pertinently, "There are too many priests in Spain. The priests and bull-fights are ruining the country by impoverishing the people. One-third of the income of the people goes toward the support of these, while the schoolmasters are ill paid or not paid at all, and many are obliged to leave Spain for South America."

IV.

The Fair Women. But not alone in the stately relic of the Alca-zen, or the Alhambra, has the Saracen left a like distinguishable and distin-guished mark. In the personal beauty of the lovely Madrileñas on the Prado, of the Sevillian water-carrier, and of the Cordovian coquette on the low balcony overhanging the garden, the Moor, with that quality manifestly his own, has left a trace irradicable, and as harmonious with the surroundings as could be divined. The curve of the lips, the oriental perfection at the temples, the perfect tapering of the white, undimpled chin, and the speaking eyes in whose myste-

rious mazes lie countless histories of the heart, each in itself a distinct trace of its noble lineage and in perfect consonance with its counterpart, these qualities of the Spanish beauty are expressively redolent of the high type of humanity which so splendid an era of civilization could but achieve. Gautier records from a French point of view, De Amicis from an Italian, Schmidt-Weissenfels from a German, and Sunset Cox from an American, the transcendent lovliness of the dark-eyed Spanish maid, and in a more or less degree of fervency and poetical spirit—for what man could write prosaically upon so trenchant and hearty a subject?—attempt to commit to hard, cold paper the divine revelations of one glance of the Spanish maiden's eyes. But there is a delightful consonance of opinion with regard to the chief charms and the causes of their being. That exquisite, almost divine femininity, first of all, which gives the most noble of womanly dignity alike to my lady of the alameda promenade, to the peasant girl concerned with the homely duties of the husbandman's hut, and to the deft young toiler of the tobacco factories ; and second, the complexions, which are unparalled in clearness, texture and susceptibility, to the finest shades of feeling, betraying to the keen thought-reader the depth of the stir within the heart which is so archly dissembled. The cause of the first, that Murillo-like purity of heart, coupled with an aspect of womanly strength, is perhaps the excessive reserve of the sexes, and the lack of knowledge of men and the worldly side of life ; the source

of the second quality of beauty, the
complexion, is without doubt the sunshine, which in northern climates, with
our modern caprices of artificial life,
ruins complexions.

V.

The Fortress. We went from here to
the Guadalquivir River,
where it is crossed by an old bridge
built by the Romans and reconstruct-
ed by the Arabs. On the other end
of the bridge is seen an old fortress,
called Clalhora Towers. Several old
Moorish mills were pointed out to us,
one of which is still in use. The hills
across the river, we were told, were once
the site of a prosperous city, although
now it is a desert waste and nothing remains of ancient Cordova, but the relics.
On this side of the river is the new Cordova. "If we are to credit the state-
ments of Moorish chroniclers," says Mc-
Clintock, "at the end of the ninth century Cordova had a population of one
hundred thousand, and was the successful rival of Bagdad and Damascus, and

the home of literature and art. Whereas, now few traces of its former magnificence remain."

Of course, the morning found us anxious to visit the ancient Alcazar which is held to be little inferior to the Alhambra of Granada. The Alcazar was repaired, and the greater part of it was rebuilt, by Peter the Cruel. We walked through the halls and admired the wonderful Moorish ceilings and mosaic work, the combination of color and light being ever a source of new enjoyment. The gardens at the rear of the Alcazar were laid out in cinquecento style by the famous gardeners of Charles V., and are most beautiful.

Through groves of flowering date palms one hundred feet high, down the narrow avenues of orange trees laden with fruit, and between beds of rare flowers and hedges of myrtle, we made our way, enchanted by the luxurious tropical plants, and the enlivening scenes about us.

VI.

Cordova as a Relic. One of the most ancient of cities, and abounding too in records of all the races that have made, fought for it, and dwelt in it during the last twenty centuries, it should be very picturesque, very delapidated, and full of artistic treasures. These last have almost entirely disappeared ; and for the rest, it is bright and clear, and at times indeed, quite ordinary, and as immaculate as prosaic whitewash can make it. They say that a thousand years ago it had a million inhabitants, with three hundred mosques, nine hundred baths, and six hundred fountains. It may have been so ; but there is now, oddly enough, but little evidence of any such greatness. The report reminds one irresistibly of the two millions of men of King Agrican's army, whom Orlando killed with his own hand, according to the ballad. The great bridge—the *Puerte Viejo*—one of the earliest records of the Moors in Spain, built upon old Roman foundations very soon after Rod-

erick's discomforture at the Gaudelete,
is of much interest. The heavy Doric
gateway, that guards the entrance to
the town from the bridge, is a characteristic piece of Herreros genius, and if
the relics upon it are by Torrigiaro,
they are in no way worthy of the man
who wrought the San Geronimo in Seville museo, or Henry the Seventh's se-
sepulcher in Westminster Abbey. The
whole mosque is a marvelous building,
and unique. It is huge and fairy-like
withal, lovely in detail, and wonderful
in the perfection of its avenues and lines
of columns. In fact, it is anything you
please, except just what it should be, as
a great religious house—imposing. Now
and then in some corner, where the view
is contracted, and where a group of
kneeling, black-robed penitents induces
a much-needed dwarfing of humanity,
there may be formed some notion of
what the place was in its better days:
after its enlargement; that is to say,
when the *Mihrab*, (meaning "place in-
habited by the Spirit of God", as this
was the holy spot to which the Moslems
turned in prayer, and where the sacred

books were kept) had just been added,
and the *Pratio de los Maranjos* finished ;
when there was as yet no need of windows, but all these avenues of delicate
columns within opened straight upon
the even more lovely and exactly corres-
ponding avenues of orange trees without ; before *Almanzor* had added the
eight eastern naves ; before an obtrusive
Renaissance had been thrust down in
the center, and where in place of the
bald, mean vaulting there was fine arte-
sonado work of sweet-smelling woods.
Now, however, when the place has been
shorn of all its beauty of proportion,
shorn too of the old rites and the old life,
it is grievously hard to get over the notion that one is in an exaggerated crypt.

VII.

The Great Mosque.   The Mosque of Cordova is the most important
of the many examples of Moorish architecture in Spain, for the reason that it
represents the *Alpha*, as it were, while
the Alhambra represents the *Omega*, of
Saracenic achievements in art. The

many rulers who held successive dominion over the land upon which it
stands, augmented the several parts of
the main structure from time to time by
specimens of the progress in the styles
current in the realm, down to the overthrow of the dominion. With Caliph
Abd-el-Rahman as the builder of its
foundations, and the Christian kings
who turned it into a sanctuary of Catholic worship, as vandals whose restora-
tions need sorely to be restored, this
Mosque is the Rosetta Stone—the key
to all the intermediate reigns by which
we interpret the evolution of the noble
spirit of art, which produced the marvels of Granada. Hesham, Caliph
Hakeem, El Mansour, down to the discovery of America and the overthrow of
the Moorish provinces in the most brilliant reign of Ferdinand and Isabella,
scarcely one king missed an opportunity of leaving an indelible trace upon
this matchless testimonial. Not alone
then as a noble archive upon which is
enrolled the historical evolution of
Moorish art, is the building of interest;
but as a living chronicle of the succes-

sive eras contemporary with its many developments.

We walked through the Plaza Major, a public court where, formerly, Jews, heretics and atheists were tortured and burned in the *Auto-da-fes.* Bull fights used to be given here, and young noblemen, to show their valor, would attack ferocious bulls, in order to gain favor with their mistresses who looked on from the balconies above.

In a book called " The History of the Female Sex," the following is related : " The greatest and most dangerous proof of love in a man was to fight a wild bull in honor of his mistress. Cavaliers begged permission of their ladies to engage in these fights. During the conflict the ladies waved their handkerchiefs in token of approbation ; and when the cavaliers had vanquished their antagonists, they made a low obeisance to the objects of their passion, and kissed the sword with which they had killed or mortally wounded the bull. These fights, in honor of their ladies, cost many a Spanish gentleman his life. A few days before Madam D'Ouroy visited

Spain, a young cavalier heard that some of the most ferocious bulls of the mountains were taken and were kept for an approaching fight.

This intelligence inspired the intrepid youth with the wish to acquire honor for himself and his intended bride in an engagement with one of these formidable animals. He acquainted his mistress with his design, and she by the most affecting entreaties, endeavored to dissuade him from his purpose. All her prayers and all her remonstrances were in vain. Athirst for glory, the lover entered the lists with others of his own rank and age, and encountered one of the first bulls that were let loose. The fight had hardly begun, when a stranger advanced in the dress of a peasant, and with a dart gave the bull a painful wound. Quitting his first antagonist, the furious animal rushed upon his new adversary, whom he immediately overwhelmed with a mortal blow upon the ground. In falling, the long and beautiful hair of the youth was exposed by the loss of his cap, and it appeared that the uninvited enemy of the wounded bull

was a young female, and the bride of
the cavalier who had determined to
fight in honor of her. The bridegroom,
rendered desperate by this spectacle, de-
fended his mistress, bathed in blood
with astonishing heroism. He likewise
received several mortal wounds. The
unfortunate lovers were placed in the
same chamber, where, at their request,
the nuptial ceremony was performed,
and in a few hours they both expired.

IX.

The Beggars.   The Cordovan beggar, like the Cordovan
beauty, is a part and parcel of glory and
the distinction of the realm. What
would be these narrow, murky streets,
were it not for these qualifying and
characteristic sweepings of the society—
the outcast sons of nobles in rags, that
bear out the dignity of princedom, the
metropolitan daughters of the great
queen of loyal consistency with her surroundings : Ruin ? These tattered and
unsandaled courtiers at the great shrine
of beggary, these kings turned paupers

in fact, yet king were in nature, these
splendid usurpers of the clean, clear air
which they deem that even God thanks
them for exhaling, these keen-witted,
diplomatic, legendary dogs in the foreign
footsteps, who follow and solicit alms as
if they but sought to do the stranger .
honor in accepting his gratuities—surely
here does mendicancy wear a most interesting feature, and to be interesting
in our time is to be inspired. I have
never been annoyed by beggars, never
allowing myself to lose my temper for
their impertinence, nor to lose my interest in the refined arts and happy siz-
ing up of human nature to know just
where to strike, and when. But here, I
am often astonished at the *finesse* of the
science of exhortation, delightfully in-
sulted now and then, but never weary
of watching the rapidity with which
rôle after rôle will be assumed by the
mendicant, all equally effectual, yet
seeming to the unfortunate beggar
equally unavailing. The beggars of
Spain—witted, manly rascals that they
are—while not escaping my maledic-
tions, do not escape my interest, my ad-

miration, and—my pennies. I would
wish · to endue them, but at the same
moment wonder what would become of
Spain without its beggars?—disgust-
ingly commonplace, like a flat country
with but here and there a flower, a tree,
· or a cloud to break the neutral monotony, but no mountains, no lowlands,
nor icy peaks, nor broad rivers, and
alas!—more noble and inspiring than
all—no lustre in the eyes of the mendicant at the wayside, nor compassionate
beauty of soul in the face of the fair
young Cordovan maid who halts her
chaperon long enough to drop a blessing into the heart, and a penny into the
hat, of the crouching caricature she
brushes with her tiny slipper.

Seville

III.

" ' Dicár y panchabár,' sata penda Manjaró Lillar."—
Gypsy proverb.

" ' To see and to believe.' as St. Thomas says."

" The sword ! the sovereign sword !—
    By Allah does it lift the plain,
    By Allah and the holy word,
      Crush mountains to the vales again.

' The sword ! the sun-bright sword !
    Go ask the East, the South, the West,
    Who rules? 'Tis I, thy sovereign, lord—
      Right hand of God, by him thrice blest ! "
From the relics of the unhappy King Alkahem.

SEVILLE.

I.

The Classic City. Seville bears the wholesome resemblance to an oriental city which one looks for in this land of the departed Moor. One feels that he is approaching Bagdad, the spires and minarets of the Cathedral, once a mosque, the Alcazar, and the dotting of fiercely blazing domes everywhere, give evidence of a city of imposing interest. The city of Murillo! is not this in itself enough to touch the heart to new activity? For once the enthusiasm which is inspired of Velas-

quez, and the famous studio in the
palace of his sovereign, and the recalling
with delight the handiwork of the great
master, is forgotten in the thought that
here, in the very place of his birth and
hermitage, the genius of Murillo shall
meet face to face. Seville is the most
versatile of cities in the character of its
attractions.   First, its great mosques,
admired by Longfellow ; its museum of
Murillos, admired by Cunningham ; its
fruit, extolled by Byron ; its Roman
ruins, expatiated upon by de Amicis ;
and last of all, the chiefest delight
which should have been first in our
catalogue, the Sevillian ladies, extolled,
admired, written and talked about, under
every star of the firmament.

All night and early morning, along
the winding Guadalquiver, through
orchards of olives and great hedges of
cacti, the whole distance from Cordova,
and occasionally an orchard of pomegranates in bloom. Our guide, a native
of Morroco, takes us through the narrow streets, which are covered with awnings to keep them in shade and protect
them from the hot sun. Everywhere we

see great crowds of people filling the
streets, coming in holiday attire from
city and country, to see the procession
and celebration of Corpus Christi day.
Excursions have come in from the
country and cities adjoining, as Seville
has the reputation of having the grandest
Corpus Christi celebration in the world.
There were four thousand soldiers in
line ; the archbishop and all the canons,
priests and students, the city governor
and officers, twelve men bearing the
different saints upon massive silver
and gold altars, and caskets and orna-
ments loaded with beautiful flowers,
started out to march through the narrow streets from the cathedral at ten
o'clock, and they must return to it pre-
cisely at twelve o'clock. The balconies
and windows on the high buildings
were full of people, and flowers and
evergreens were stretched upon the
pavements below, so that the streets
were literally covered with them, and
after the procession had passed, men
were engaged in sweeping the streets
and gathering the flowers in bunches.
The ladies all wore black silk dresses,

with veils or mantillas thrown over their heads.

After the procession comes the bull-fight, for which great preparations are made, as the bull-fights of Seville are noted on account of the great dexterity of the performers.

The champion bull-fighter of Spain was a fellow passenger on our train, and he seemed to draw a crowd around him just as any of our noted prize-fighters would in America. Our guide showed us the street on which the bull-fighters live. They seem to form an aristocracy of their own. Some of the most skilful get very large salaries for their services. A daughter of one of these bull-fighters was married in the cathedral a short time ago, and the Bishop and aristocracy of the city were present.

II.

The Cathedral.

Our first explicit duty was to visit the Cathedral, the site of which was once occupied by a temple of Venus Salambo, at one time the fashionable deity of the

Sevillians. This gave way to a splendid Mosque, on the plan of the one at Cordova. After this came the second and last Mosque, built by Emir Yusuf in 1184. The chapter then met and decided on erecting a church, "so large and beautiful that coming ages may proclaim us mad to have undertaken it." The old building was converted into a cathedral by St. Ferdinand. It is fast going to ruin, and last August a large part of the ceiling fell. The old cathedral is underpinned and braced up by heavy framework. The government is trying to restore it, which, it is said, will require thirty years. Nothing remains of the old mosque but the lower part of the beautiful Giralda Tower, the Court of the Oranges, and a portion of the outer walls.

III.

The Giralda. Not the least pleasing architectural surprise of Seville is this famous Giralda, the campanile which either celebrates the victories of King Yousouf, at Alarcos, in

the year 1159, or else an observatory of
that distinguished patron of the astrolo-
gists, history disputes which ; but standing quite alone amid the superb flowering palms, which, although of immense
height, only prove the loftiness of the
tower itself, it is a noble piece of Saracenic art. The Pseudo Saracenic clas-
sicism of the belfry only bewilders us in
our endeavor to restore, with certainty,
the original termination which was displaced by this stupid caprice of Ferdinand Riaz in 1568, which, though it
increases the height of the tower some
ninety feet, leaves us in doubt as to what
skill the Saracens may have displayed
thereon. Compared with this tower,
the companile on the piazza of St. Mar-
co, at Venice, which was distinctly contemporary, is very bald, and without
those engaging qualities of religious enthusiasm with which the Moslem inspired the perfection of his places of
worship or monuments of religious war.

The outskirts of the city present the
more truly Spanish spirit of the place,
for there, by the huge, gloomy walls, the

city and country meet and exchange
wares and little glimpses of each other's
world. Little groups of countrymen,
with their lazy donkeys at their heels,
stand here and there, bickering over
some trifle, and then exchanging the
latest gossip, or expatiating upon some
political event in which they all make
severest effort to be considered learned.
These little groups represent the forum
and debating ground of the Radical or
Conservative who justifies his cause by
the success of his donkey-load of produce, and for pictures of true Spanish
life, are unequalled.

Granada

V.

" Helo, helo por do viene
  El Moro por la calzada," etc.

" Look you ! hither on the highway
   Comes the mounted Moorish knight ;
  Rising in his golden stirrups,
   On his palfrey, snowy white.

  Buskins of morocco leather,
   Spurs of silver, mien severe ;
  On his front a stately emblem,
   In his hand a flashing spear !' "
                    From an old Ballad of the Cid.

" Where in the proud Alhambra's ruined breast,
  Barbaric monuments of pomp repose."
                    Scott's Don Roderick.

GRANADA.

I.

The Renowned City Granada at last!
What an absorbing pic-
ture !—what a detailed legend, sweeter
in its impressive mystery—the mere hints
and glimpses of a most lustrous age—
than all the chronicles of the eras. The
lofty walls, the eyeless watch-ports, the
worm-eaten portals which swing back
with a groan that proves us favored, the
silent ramparts with the happy spread
of wild anemone, and poppy, and iris at
their base, all opening out to the applauding sunshine !

II.

The Scenes.   Our hotel, " The Washington Irving," which instantly flatters the American heart with a sense of nearness, and breaks down the barriers of formality, as it were, stands at the base of the very Alhambra walls. In the cool of the morning, awakened by the swallows and the cries of the ware-mongers in the still streets, we throw open the blinds, for the first time surveying the old walls of the famous citadel at our right, while on the opposite side stretch away the fair gardens of the ancient villa. In the luxuriance of this almost tropical morning, we hasten along the wide avenue, where the waters of the mountain rush down on either side and leap a cascade with a roar of triumph, and pass through an old Moorish archway. Beyond us the walls of grayish neutral tints stand ragged and toothed against the luminous sky, and below, the gardens, where the early sun makes more resplendent the ancient palaces which, through all

the dust and ignoble dissuetude of ages,
bear the impress of their nobility. Then
the great palace of the Alhambra itself
greets us, and from this distance, in the
clear light, we note the wild flowers and
trailing garlands wreathing about the
base of the dignified old portals, as if
conspiring to conceal the wounds in the
side of this noble testament of history.
Then we happen upon a cluster of little
children, dressed like pretty puppets
ready for some kingly pantomine, and
we step back to observe them in their
happy *naiveté*, which our presence would
quickly dispel. How bright and animated are the pretty "joy-children" in
their gorgeous jackets of such sparkle
and color, against the cold, clammy
tints of the venerable monuments at
each hand, of which they are so heedless! Then pressing on, with an eye to
the surprises of the solemn place, we
come upon the great portal which con-
fronts us like a revelation. Above and
about it are those interminable mazes of
arabesques, mosaics of wreaths, cuni-
form tracings, rosettes and hundred-
cornered stars—all spread out like a rich

mantle hung over the portal in honor
of the great king who first passed the
threshold, and which convinces us that
we are about to press the most sacred
and historical stones of the whole Saracenic dominion.   Then from hall to hall,
from court-room to the baths, from
harem to assembly, we loiter at will, enchanted with the ever-changing vista
through the bewildering mazes of marble and mosaic : the old city, the distant
valleys, dotted here and there with the
white villas, and the two torrent rivers
rushing down through the great city,
the. whole dazzling picture framed
by the fiercely white peaks of the ice-
clad Sierra Nevadas, which stand bold
and ragged against the transparent blue
heavens.   How perfect the *ensemble*, how
exquisite every detail !   What an art
was that of the Arab, and what a devotion brought out its absolute perfection, whereby, excluding nature in her
outward forms, the whole sense is
feasted with these intermingling fan-
tasies of arabesques, dazzling with their
flashing contrasts, yet never forcing in-
harmonies upon the eye ; and all set in

a frame of such massive, neutral masonry, that it gives full force and beauty
to each of the several parts, uniting them
into a concrete and perfect whole.

III.

The Festa.　　　Feasted to satiety at
last, we go down into the
old city, to return again to the noble
structure when the novelty has somewhat worn away, and the enthusiasm of
first impressions may yield to an intellectual survey of the period contemporary with this perfection of Moorish art.
This is a *festa*-day, as they would say in
Italy, and crowds from all quarters are
congregating, preparatory to holding
two important events in Spanish life—a
fair and a bull-fight.   In a dark, narrow
street we stumbled fortunately upon the
old cathedral where Ferdinand and Isabella lie side by side, beneath their elaborate monuments.   We were not a little
impressed with the solemnity of the place,
in view of the fact, that they who were
paying respectful deference to the shrine
of the monarchs, were sons of the very
land whose discovery was consummated

by the largess at their hands—the very
land upon which they never set foot.
If they could see their developed
prodigy to-day, with her sixty-five millions of free souls, with her republican
independence of all the world else, with
her wealth, her educational resources,
her religious and material interests,
what wonder and surprise would over-
whelm them !

The crowds about the streets that lead
to the fair and the bull-fight are motley
and picturesque in the extreme, the
women in most strange incongruities
of color, with crimson or yellow shawls
thrown carelessly over their black hair,
and the men in peasant costume, with
scarlet sashes at the waist.

IV.

The Gypsies. On Monday morning we
were conducted down the
fine avenue which takes us around
Mount Sacro, where the scene is most
impressive, the Vega winding through
the valley below, and beyond us the numerous villas, or *carinenas*, as they are

called in Granada, with their gardens of
roses, cypress and myrtle, with the old
city and its cathedral at our right.
Shortly we come upon those characteristic portions of Spanish life—the caves
in the mountain rocks, which are inhab-
ited by the gypsies. Upon the invita-
tion of a rather pretty young gypsy girl,
we entered one of their hovels, but were
satisfied with a superficial glance, and
were content to beat a hasty retreat
to the tune of a yelping cur at our heels.
The bed was in a dark room, close to
the damp rocks, and beyond these small

chambers were innumerable others, apparently, with plenty of children, curs, pigs and chickens, holding one another in terms of great familiarity. I was told that our entering the caves was rather a dangerous proceeding, as the occupants are notorious for their thieving propensities; but I treated them with courtesy, and gave them the *paseta*, which put their acquisitive passions to rest.

V.

The Alhambra. Again and again we visit the Alhambra, never tiring of its splendor, but rather more and more seriously impressed. Through the massive halls, so silent and imposing, we press, ever more and more astonished with the perfection of every detail. One large, magnificent room, which looks out over the city and the stretch of hills beyond, is the " Assembly Room," where was discussed, four hundred odd years ago, the momentous subject of Columbus' discoveries, and the consent of the king and queen given

to the brave explorer and his followers.
Then comes the harem—enchanting
spot, so full of romance, misery, and unbounded interest, where the dark-eyed
favorites of the Caliph peeped through
the open lattice ; and then, too, the
marble bath-rooms beyond, where those
aspiring gallants, who were ambitious
to gaze upon the faces of the beautiful
maidens in captivity, expatiated their
crimes at this very fountain-side, where
the discoloration, they would have us to
believe, marks the flow of their life-
blood. Well said Charles the Fifth, that
inglorious vandal, who, like the rest of
the ignoble Spanish kings, could not
bear to die and leave no finger-marks on
this magnificent testament to keep his
memory green—a royal autograph fiend
—well said he of Boabdil, the Moorish
king, "I would rather have made this
Alhambra my sepulchre than to have
lived without a kingdom in the Al-
puxarras ! "

As for history, the Alhambra was begun in the year 1248, with a view to ri-
valling the architectural splendors of
Bagdad and Damascus, and both were

finished by Mahommed II. Under
Ferdinand and Isabella, the monks and
soldiers who were left in and around the
Mosques and fortresses of the hated
Moors, vented their spite upon this
splendid treasure which the fleeing
owners could not bear away with them.
This, with the vandalism of the fifth
Charles, and that of the French under
Napoleon, who turned the magnificent
structure into barracks for their troops,
has left many parts hopelessly despoiled.
To Signor Don Rafael Coutreras, the
celebrated architect, a native of Granada,
who still lives in the palace, is due the
legitimate restoration of many parts, at
the instance of the court. "In the Alhambra everything interests us," says
Lomas, "for besides the intrinsic value
as a monument, how many poetical legends of love and war, how many as-
sociations has it, with stirring scenes of
harem dramas, political intrigues and
bloody executions !" The taste, the refined elegance, the wonderful variety,
the airy lightness and veil-like trans-
parency of filagree, stucco, contrasts of
color and gilt, like the sides of a Stam-

boul casket—all this proves that the caliphs of Granada who held dominion over the sunny land which their poets defined as a "terrestial Paradise," were of a race of men of high and well-balanced intellect.

VI.

Arab Genius. And while resting ourselves by the beautiful fountain in the famous Court of Lyons, let us dwell for a moment upon the striking illustrative qualities which this facile, brilliant, yet skin-deep beauty of architecture and design gives evidence —qualities so consonant with the Moor, so impossible to the Egyptian, the Budhist, the Japanese. How does this surface brilliancy pale before the vast mental picture of the ruins of Sarnac, of the temple of Ai at Baalbek, of the great Taj of Agra—all massive, ponderous pieces of engineering, which endure with the ages! The Mahommedan is a fatalist—eminently so. "Now!" is his holy watchword. He is of all else a creature of to-day. His arts are the fine arts, the

delicate arts, the perfect arts. He can
carve a cameo, dares even

" To paint the lily
Or throw a perfume on the violet,"

but he never attempts the mighty, the
heroic, the Titanic. He leaves that for
a northern race, whose foremost men
have less delicacy, less refinement of
touch, but a more extended view of the
world, of the universe, of God, of nature
--a more expansive idea. The Arab was
content to embrace with his perfect art a
single idea ; for the northern type—the
Newton, the Goethe, the Carlyle—the
bounds of heaven and earth are confines
indeed to their splendid presumptions
and their achievements. The circle of
the former's intellectual idea was as a
nutshell to an apple. His horizon was
the bounds of his courtyard, while the
man's of the North was the nineteen miles
of the mariner's at sea. Yet, how well—
how transcendently perfected was this little talent ! The court of Lyons in marble
—how absurd! To cover over rich and
perfect stone, dignified enough in itself,
with these dazzling arabesques, would be
" wasteful and ridiculous excess."   The

stucco demanded this embellishment to give it a dignity equal to marble—not to imitate it, indeed, but to produce something wherein the labor of the hand would vie with the ponderous and per-

fect simplicity of stone. This marvelously embellished stucco can no more be compared with marble, than the illuminated parchment of the Benedictines can be compared with the stone hieroglyphics of Thebes; each is characteristic of the distinctive period, and is perfect in itself.

VII.

Fatalism. And so, everywhere
through this gorgeous
land of the displaced Moor and the
Goth, triumphant fatalism takes prece
dence. The Romans were the last to
believe in the absolute perpetuity of
their dominion. Before them, the
Greeks believed it, and so did they of
the " chosen land," when Ezekiel pro-
phesied that the Jews " should never be
without a king." We, in our times, are
convinced of the perpetuity of our republican forms, and lay plans accord-
ingly, like those in the far past ; but
they of the middle ages were of no such
theory. The past they held in little
reverence, despoiling the cherished temples and palaces of their conquested
countries to heap up the incongruities
that the Alcazar of Cordova, and St.
Marks, of Venice, are specimens—con-
glomorations of vandalism from all
captive climes. Neither had they a
thought of the future, as the Court of
Lyons bears witness. Christianity and

climate has much to do with our reverence for the past, with our vital regard
for the future. The Arab is a creature
of superb illusions, and what is more, he
is perfectly aware that they *are* illusions.

I merely venture this much to make
plain the difference between the Arab
who makes and enjoys, and the American who criticises, and *thinks* he enjoys
the exquisite sensualism of these surroundings. We are altogether too
serious as a nation ever to give rein to
our imaginative faculties in real life.
The Arab would come into this beautiful place with his robe and pipe and
hashish, and dream away the years of a
Methusalah in perfect serenity. Lock
up an American here with the spectre of
the stock markets haunting his mind,
and he would be one of the most miserable of men.

VIII.

The Generalife. We visited the celebrated summer-palace of the
Caliphs, the Generalife, which at the
end of an ascending avenue of tall

cypress trees, overlooks the city from an
imposing eminence. The waters from
the Sierra Nevada come rushing down

through the gardens, keeping up the
ceaseless gush of fountains, the luxuriant

foliage of the tall evergreens above form-
ing an arch of matchless beauty. Orange
trees, laden with fruit are deftly trained
to spread their branches over the walls
—an uncommon horticultural conceit,
and very attractive—and beyond is the
famous court of cypresses, in the midst
of which a beautiful fountain is playing.

IX.

An old Convent. In the afternoon we
took a carriage to visit
the old convent La Cartaja. On our
way we stopped at the "mad house," as
our guide calls it, built by Charles V.,
though we did not care to enter it. It
was enough to see the wan, pinched
faces of the wretched inmates through
the grated windows, and hear their
mournful ravings. We met a group of
boys in the court, who beset us as only
Spanish beggars can, and could scarcely
make our way through them to the
foundling hospital, with its sixty babes,
which have been received into the care
of the institution without any questions
being asked. Shortly before our visit

the little ones had been weighed, bathed,
dressed and nursed, and put into tiny
little cradles, covered with clean white
linen and mosquito bars, and at our approach were apparently asleep ; but as
soon as good Mother Superior entered,
quite a number made their wants known
in a vigorous way.

From this point we climbed a steep
hill to the old church and monastery,
and were shown a large number of
paintings of great size by Cotan, the
celebrated Monkish painter and sculptor.
Most of these atrocious things represent
the persecution of the Catholics by the
Protestants in England. We went into
the chapel and saw a gorgeously furnished hall, equal to anything in the
Alhambra. On all sides were variously
colored marbles from the Sierra Nevada
mountains, precious mosaics and various
pieces of furniture built into the wall
and inlaid with silver, ebony, mother-of-
pearl and precious stones. All this prodigious work, we were told, was done by
the artist monk Cotan. We were informed that there were ninety-one
churches and chapels in Granada.

They are located on the steep hills, and are most difficult of access, but they are very attractive in their location and old style of ˙architecture, and while commanding beautiful prospects, are themselves most flattering to the surroundings.

From thence we went down into the city to see the illumination of colored lamps, it being *fête* time, and the city was decorated with arches, festoons, flowers, and other ornamentations. The grand promenade is boardered by arches and colored glass globes, illuminated from within, the contrast with the green leaves being very beautiful.

X.

The Cathedral. We were very much interested in the Cathedral Capillo de los Reyes, where are the tombs of Ferdinand and Isabella, to see the casket of beautiful jewels which the good queen, who had so fierce a fight to assist Columbus, had pawned in order to enable the explorer to venture out into the great unknown West. The king was a devout Catholic, desiring to do everything for the glory of God ; but he could see no glory in so apparently fool-hardy a project as that of the pauper Columbus. In the Sierra Nevada mountains we were shown the pass where Columbus was intercepted after the refusal of the ambassadors to assist him, and from which place he was brought back to court at the instance of the queen. It gives a startling reality to the horribly capricious times of the reign of the priest-yoked Ferdinand and his well-meaning queen. Had Columbus not accomplished his will with the vacillating queen, and had left it to others to make the discoveries, who can say what form of government, religion or social state would now be the existing fact in the place of our glorious commonwealth ?

XI.

The Donkeys.

T h e donkeys are a great "institution" in Spain ; we see them everywhere loaded with brick, stone, gravel, lumber, market stuff, or wood, and the great lazy Spaniard rides up the steep hills on his donkey's back, with his legs reaching to

the ground. On Sunday we saw a
model soda fountain. We met a Spaniard on the back of a donkey covered all
over with evergreens. On meeting a
girl who asked for his wares, the pur-
veyor dismounted, and
we stopped to watch the
proceedings. He took a
little box out of his
pocket, opened it, and
poured out into the
young girl's hand a
white powder resem-
bling soda. This the
girl put into her mouth,
while the man touched
a faucet which seemed
to protrude from the
donkey's side, and drew
water from the pig-skin demijohns
—there was one on each side of the
donkey—and handed it to her to put into
her mouth to dissolve the soda. She gave
him two cents. The water for the cities
is carried about in this way to sell, and
the street women cry out "Aqua!
Aqua!" This water is drawn from the
Alhambra wells.

XII.

The Flowers.   On our way southward,
the usual inundation of
wild flowers along the valleys gave way
to hedges of tall cacti in infinite variations of form and color, often conceal-
ing the tracts they enclosed so effectively
and shutting out our views of country
life as we advanced.   The farmers were
harvesting their grain, in the manner
which might not have surprised their
quiet grandfathers a dozen removes back,
so primitive and laborious it seemed to
me after the wonderful machines we
have in America.   Still, the glimpses we
were privileged now and then were
highly picuresque, the women in their
gaudy short frocks, and the men with
crimson sashes, both plying the sickle
with regular stroke and a movement
which is so characteristic, that it is
doubtless handed from father to son,
like the sweep of the oar of the Venetian
gondolier.

It is with regret then, heatfelt and
earnest, that we take our departure for
the south, leaving the marvellous old

cities of the painters, the poets, the historians, and the knights of romance and fact, bearing away with us a reverence for the brilliancy of Velasquez for his treasures in Madrid ; for Murillo for his treasures in Seville ; the Alhambra and its treasures in Grenada, and for the Cid, that marvellously clever knight, for his treasures in the coffer of Burgos—the coffer which secured him a huge loan from the Jews to pay for his daring exploits, and which, upon being unlocked, was found to contain, not gold and silver, not diamonds and lapis-lazuli, but an armful of bricks carefully pillowed on a bag of sand.

COFRE DE EL CID

IV.

From Granada to the South.   Our journey from Granada to Malaga, save a delight in the scenery, was not the occasion of any special mental note-taking. We halted for a few hours at the City of Boabdilla, named after the last great king of the Moors, Boabdil, who was overthrown by King Ferdinard in 1492. By alleged infringement of compact entered into at the time of his captivity, he gave up all his rights and possessions for a sum of money and repaired to Morocco. He was accused of treachery by the Moors, and of having been bribed by Ferdinand ; but Washington Irving defends him from anything of this kind, and finds nothing in all history to authorize these imputations. This king, however, was the last of the Moors in Spain after centuries of rule. To quote

the eloquent passage from Irving
apropos of this interesting period :

" The Moslem empire in Spain was but
a brilliant exotic, that took no permanent
root in the soil which it embellished.
Never was the annihilation of a people
more complete than was that of the
Morocco Spaniards. Where are they ?
Ask the shores of Barbery and its desert
places. They have not even left a distinct name behind them, though for
eight centuries they were a distinct people. A few broken monuments are all
that remain to bear witness of their
power and dominion, as solitary rocks
left far in the interior bear testimony to
the extent of some inundation. Such
is Alhambra ; a Moslem pile in the midst
of a Christian land ; an oriental palace
amidst the gothic edifices of the West ;
an elegant memento of a brave, intelligent and graceful people who conquered and ruled, and passed away."

On the way to Malaga the road is
marvellously circuitous and full of surprises at every bend. Tunnel after tunnel we rushed through to be greeted
suddenly with a new and charming vista

of gardens and vineyards, and sweeping
groves of orange, lemon and pomegranate. How in contrast were these
fair Edens to the waste, solitary deserts
of the wilderness of Spain! At Malaga,
the quaint Spanish seaport, we were
pleased to meet Col. Marston, the popular American consul. He is a brother-
in-law of Judge Lawrence, of Ohio.
The consul delighted us by taking us to
the villa of the Marquis of Loring, a
Bostonian, who received his title from
the Spanish government on account of
his success in building railroads in Spain.
He married a Spanish lady, and has ac-
cumulated a very large fortune. His
villa is most delightfully situated on the
mountain side, the water rushing down
over murmurous cascades through his
immense gardens, watering his tropical
plants which are rare and in great profusion. Nearly every plant which we at
home nourish with great care in our
greenhouses, here grows to immense
height in the open air.

The Keep of Gibral- The great rock and
tar. impregnable E n g l i s h
fortress of Gibraltar was a point that
gave us much pleasure. The approach
to the island is imposing indeed, and I
can vouch for the enthusiasm of the
early Moorish writers when they affirm,
as did Al Makkari, " That it looks like a
watch-tower in the midst of the sea," or,
as another writes, " like a mountain of
fire set in the blue waters." We sailed
about the bay, surveying the great rock
from all points. The thickly populated
hamlet that clings to the base of the rock,
looks like a terraced city, streets reced-
ing one above the other. The red coats of
the English are everywhere, and we
wonder not that old England feels proud
of her possession of such an invincible
fortress for the protection of her ships *en
voyage* to and from India. We met English faces constantly—faces so coldly in
contrast with the dark, Spanish countenance of the people across the straits,
and the angular, Moorish feature of the
African beyond. The great rock is tun-

neled with winding passages which they
call galleries. They are several miles
long, and along the outer edge the huge
guns, some weighing a hundred tons,
point in every direction through holes in
the rock. The gunners are thus perfectly safe in case of attack.

This imposing old natural cathedral
has seen many great wars and triumphs.
To the Moor and Spaniard is it particularly redolent with charms of old recol-
lections, and to English eyes it is not a
little monumental of their victories.
Within sight of this huge sentinel the
renowned Trafalgar was fought ; to the
east, Sir George Rooke was whipped ;
to the west, Rodney overturned the
Spaniards, and then came Earl St.
Vincent's victory later, and last, almost
as renowned as the first, the triumph of
Admiral Napier in 1833. To the imaginative mind what may not be seen
floating on the troubled waters that leap
up the great monster's side ? The Syrian
bark from Tyre ; the Roman trireme
from the Tiber mouth ; the galleys of
Carthage ; the caiques of the Turk,
and even the clumsy boats of the

Northmen going on pilgrimages to Israel in the twelfth century. Heroditus refers frequently to the Pillars of Hercules, as does also Strabo in his work on the Mediterranean, written contemporary with Christ. From Cadiz, so near distant, Columbus himself set sail on his second voyage for America. Thus from the earliest period this great natural fortress has been an object of historical importance. The monkeys were doubtless the first inhabitants, and there are still old conservative families of the species making sport for the inhabitants about the island. Hanno and his Carthaganian galleys on the long voyage of discovery, Timosthenes, the ally of Strabo and admiral of the fleet of Ptolemy, the merchantmen of Sidon, Tartessus and Gades, down to the men-of-war which float the flag of a newly discovered country at the huge base of the pillar—these have the generations of apes and sea-gulls, which, as in the past, now hold portions of the rock in absolute tenure, seen come and go. From Sigurd, King of Norway, who in 1109 fought here a battle with the

Pagans, while on his way to Palestine,
through all the wars of the Vigoths and
barbarians, and the later sieges in which
Nelson, Blake and Rodney distinguished
themselves severally at divers periods,
down to the last shot of the sunset gun
on the cliff and the salute of the " Lancaster," which lay at anchor as we came
down from the interior galleries of the
rock at evening, the monkeys, the *genii
loci* of the gray monumental fastness,
have been granted a peculiar privilege.

During the beautiful moonlight night,
as we lay at anchor in the harbor, we
could catch the strains of martial music
coming from the war ship in the distance.   The " Star-Spangled Banner "
roused our enthusiasm, and we gave the
good flag a cheer. We were rowed over to
the " Lancaster," and were shown about
the ship by Ensign Clark, of Ohio.   The
" boys," over four hundred in number,
were happy because they were ordered
home after a three years' cruise.   They
had been buying Moorish trumpery with
the proverbial prodigality of the sailor
on land.

Morocco

VI.

" The world is a mirror : show thyself in it. and it will
reflect thy image."—*Moorish Proverb.*

" Live with him who prays, and thou prayest ; live with
him who sings, and thou singest."—*Ibn Asad.*

I

First glimpses of the Moslem Country. We entered the bay of Tangiers, and upon our steamer casting anchor, it was surrounded by scores of small crafts, and a motley and wrangling crowd of Arab boatmen who set up an unearthly yell, and importuned us to engage their services to bear our persons and luggage to land. They were dressed in black leather, were swarthy and characteristic in complexion, and looked to us to be a totally different people from any we had seen in any part of our travels. Fortunately for us,

there was an American lady on board
who had apprised the American Consul
by telegram of her coming, and soon in
the distance we saw riding over the
waves, a trim barque bearing the stars
and stripes, approaching the ship. The
sea was running so high that it was with
the utmost difficulty that we managed
to get to shore, and not until we were
well soaked with the spray, but without
serious further injury. A great crowd of
Moors and Arabs from all parts of the
coast and interior were encamped on the
shore, awaiting the word of their com-
mander to start on the pilgrimage to
Mecca. It was an interesting sight, and
the enthusiasm was imparted to the foreign observers from the native enthusi-
asts who swelled with religious fervor
and praise. Over a thousand pilgrims
had started the day before. Even in
these days of steam and of French and
English rule in Africa, the pilgrimage to
Mecca is a long, tedious and dangerous
course. The path to the honorable desig-
nation "Hadji," which is coveted by
every pious Moslem, is far from being a
way of roses. The time of departure is

as soon as possible after the great feast which celebrates the close of the Ramadhan. Like other Mahommedan feasts, this is moveable and occurs about eleven days earlier each year. The steamers from Tangiers eastward are loaded with these Moslems. They are carried on deck and in the hold, and as the fare does not include provisions, much hardship must be endured by many of the poorer pilgrims who often sell about all their worldly possessions to raise the comparatively large sum required for the passage. On account of their filthy condition, they are not favored by the officers and cabin passengers of the vessel, as we had many occasions to note. They do a little traffic on their return in retailing to the faithful at home, sundry little curiosities of worship, scented aloe-wood and incense from the Holy City. The pilgrimage may now be accomplished in four months, from this point. Many of the older and weaker of the pilgrims die of the hardships on the road. In years of famine, or when there are reports of a quarantine in the East, few pilgrims venture; and also when the time

of the feast falls before the completion of
the harvest, for but few of those engaged
in rural occupations can leave home
to go abroad on a pious pilgrimage.
I notice by the American papers that
there is a large emigration into the United States from Algiers and Morocco.
I cannot be persuaded, however, that
they would make good American citizens.

We were, fortunately, not long de-
tained at the Custom House. The solemn, sober-browed Moors, squatting on
their mats, took things with marvelous
leisure, and only glanced at the contents
of our bags, allowing us to pass on.
Donkeys were brought us to ride through
the narrow streets to the hotel, and the
experience was anything but an exhila-
rating one. Oh, the dirt, the confusion,
the Babel of tongues, and that peculiar
ever-prevailing shriek of the Arab!

Our room at the hotel overlooked the
bay and the Moorish encampment so
wildly picturesque on the shores, and
we could see the devout Mussulmans on
the housetops holding up their arms, and
with face toward Mecca, bowing, then
falling prostrate and then rising a mo-

ment after, like curious puppets in some Eastern passion-play. We watched them interestedly for some time, and were surprised to remark the length of their devotions, which seemed interminable.

Guides and mules were procured us, and we started at once through the tortuous streets, so narrow that often those who confront us can scarcely pass. The costumes and customs of the Moors are peculiar indeed. The men in long flowing robes, white turbans, bare legs and feet, wear that patient, resigned aspect of devout persistence, as if each curious personage were revivified from the scriptural archives of the book of Job. It seemed as if it were impossible for them to carry anything in their hands or arms; for, with this neglect of their robes, the breeze would expose them at full length. The Moorish type is very pronounced, but it does not seem to me that in facial expressions they differ very strikingly one from another. Perhaps this is a noticeable fact with regard to nations so individual, and by climate and instinct so conservative—the Hindu and the Chinese, for example.

II

The women are exceed-
The Arab Women.
ingly reserved, sublimely
innocent, and indolent to a degree un-
surpassed by a tombstone, to which each
of them bears so somber a resemblance.
They wear the long white robe, very
dignified and graceful not unoften, full
white trousers fastened at the ankle,
and high-heeled slippers clinging to the
toes. Their faces, of course, are covered,
but now and then one will favor a stranger with a glimpse of the upper half of
her countenance with most bewitching

archness in the pose, leading the beholder's imagination to portray mentally the
rest of the face consistent with the
warmth and lustre of the eyes—not unoften an illusion fatal to the enchant-
ment. The veil is most consistent with
nature, feeding by ruse and art the very
flame the most impressive feature kin-
dles. The young wear the veil to
conceal their beauty, making it all the
more a prize to behold and possess; the
old wear it, likewise, that they may conceal the wrinkles and most quickly fad-
ing features, and only by that last dim-
ming grace of the human physiognomy,
the eyes, be judged. Still, one naturally
divines youth by other characteristics
—the sprightliness of the step, for instance, and shapeliness of the fingers.
Old women have, too, a set, certain way
of doing things, allowing their manners
to betray their maturity. Both old and
young among the women ride man-fash-
ion on donkeys, and certainly would not
be impressive in the ranks of cavalry.

Among the rich, woman is the certain
slave of her lord's pleasure; among the
poor, she is the household drudge and

the manufacturer of almost every convenience for daily use. Every thing is
Eastern; Eastern in climate and scenery,
in architecture, in language and conventional life. Moslemism amalgamates—
unifies. It does not permit the disunited
parts to become estranged. The great
religion is the heartstone about which
gather the tens of thousands of divers
lands and climates, yet this great lamp
permeates the depths of their individual
natures, making the dissimilar the composite. Whether in the little mosque,
crouching timidly in one corner of the
great walled city of Shanghai, or in the
superb palaces of Penang, in the rich
mosques of Colombo, Benares or Scu-
tari, there is no difference in spirit, whatever diversity of physical individuality
in the adherents — Mahommedans the
world over all turn their faces toward
Mecca.

* * *

It struck me forcibly that although it
was the Moors—the forefathers of these
very people, perhaps—who built the

superb monuments of the Alhambra and the Alcazar, here in Morocco, their own land, no vestige of a possible glory remains, and no evidence that such a glory once existed. The houses are absolutely without form or comeliness ; square blocks of whitewashed stone with small windows and stout, prison-like doors, like long rows of polished cubes piled one upon another, despairingly monotonous. But, however much one's eyes are repulsed by the ugly setting of the picture, the Moor and his family are interesting and sober studies.

The Snake-charmers and Sorcerers. We rode out to the market, or *Sok*, as it is called, and another typical African scene met our eyes—a recalling picture which brought out of the illimitable past the true spirit of the soil. It was the spectacle of the snake-charmers and the fire-eaters—marvellous magicians who call from the farthermost parts of the desert an audience of most picturesque and motley consistence. Their strange music,

more in the nature of a funeral wail,
their wild chanting and barbaric manœu-
vers of hands and arms—these, together
with the astounding feats that they per-

form, found the audience, ourselves in-
cluded, in a most applauding and
marveling mood. Notwithstanding the
fact that the open mouths of the snakes
look so ferocious, the feat loses something of its illusion by the evidence from
good authority that the fangs are torn

from the serpents ere the magicians attempt any feats of peril with them ; and
doubtless some qualifying clause of a
like order enters into the statement that
the fierce, bronzed fire-eaters really did
gulp down the livid flames which they
were advertised to do, and apparently
did with such astonishing ease.

Cafés. After a late dinner, the
same day, an Arab in·
terpreter, lantern in hand, led the way
through the narrow streets where we
were stared at immeasurably for either
our impertinence or our bravery in ven-
·turing out at night, and finally found
ourselves in a curious little Moorish
café, silent, rather plain, but full of
character, where, with a number of
natives seated on mats about, we partook
of a kind of tea served in glasses—a
beverage somewhat resembling mint, and
very sweet. The Moors were smoking
hashish, which they carried in little
pouches, in the natural hempen state,
with which they stuffed the little bowls
of their pipes. The newcomers, on ar-

riving, kicked off their slippers, as if
entering a sacred enclosure, a bit of
courtesy which corresponds to our doff-
ing our hats; and then doubling up

their legs lazily on a mat, with scarcely
a word, save an occasional " God be
with you," to an acquaintance, they be-
gan their reposeful smoke.

A native Musicale

From this familiar haunt of the Moor we went to one of his festivities which doubtless in our country would be called a *Musicale.* Five musicians, seated about an ancient looking court bearing all the dilapidation of a primeval temple, composed the orchestra with tambourines, a sort of mandolin, a two-stringed fiddle cut out of a single block of wood, and another instrument resembling a violin ; while another, a familiar face which we had seen at the Custom House, clapped his hands as an accompaniment. All in the room sang, accompanied by these wild instruments. The low, wailing, sighing chant of the wild Arab rose and fell with seemingly interminable cadence and repetition ; more suited, it was my thought, to the wild hills beyond the sight and roar of cities, around the camp fires of the Faithful. The musicians swayed their bodies with the undulations of the weird falsetto, now and then raising their eyes heavenward, as if in the keenest ecstasy of enjoyment. We cheered them lustily at the close, and received an encore in genial tribute.

The visiting of one of the Arab schools was another enjoyable feature of our stay in Morocco. The master, a solemn-faced, gray old Signor, who might have been taken for father Abraham himself, was possessed of two indispensables to his dignity as preceptor—a long, white beard and a long black stick. Every now and then he would stroke his beard with his hand, and then stroke the head of a pupil for inattention. Huge lettered quotations from the Koran were hung up near by, which scriptural injunctions were repeated in a stupid monotone by the pupils. A review of these scriptures is nearly all the education they receive. Yet they yearly turn out upon the inoffensive world, scores of young doctors of all eastern sciences, from geometry to gymnastics, and arm them with huge sealed diplomas, after the fashion of the Paduan universities.

III.

The Infidel City. Tangier the White has the appearance of being the outpost of some Mahommedan heaven, that has been abandoned by the faithful to the merciless glitter of unrespecting foreign diplomacy and cant. The Sultan abhors it, the Mahommedan deplores its subjugation under these con- quests of foreign conventions, and the native has the audacity to abandon a portion of his daily prayer-time to the inveigling of foreign gullibility. From the sea the city presents a highly pictur- esque appearance, the minarets of the mosques and the kiosks of the several harems standing out bold above the white square houses so like piles of chalk blocks freshly mined from the mountain- side, and contrasting strongly with the foreign-looking villas surrounded by pretty gardens on the outskirts. Within, the city loses much of its glory, as does every southern seaport which has the clear atmosphere, the intensely blue sky, the green and luxurious hills beyond, and the dark wild sea beneath for a handsome setting to so capital a picture. Once within, the eye is always interested, seldom excited, and never enchanted. The glamour goes, the flavor of the wine not proving its quality.

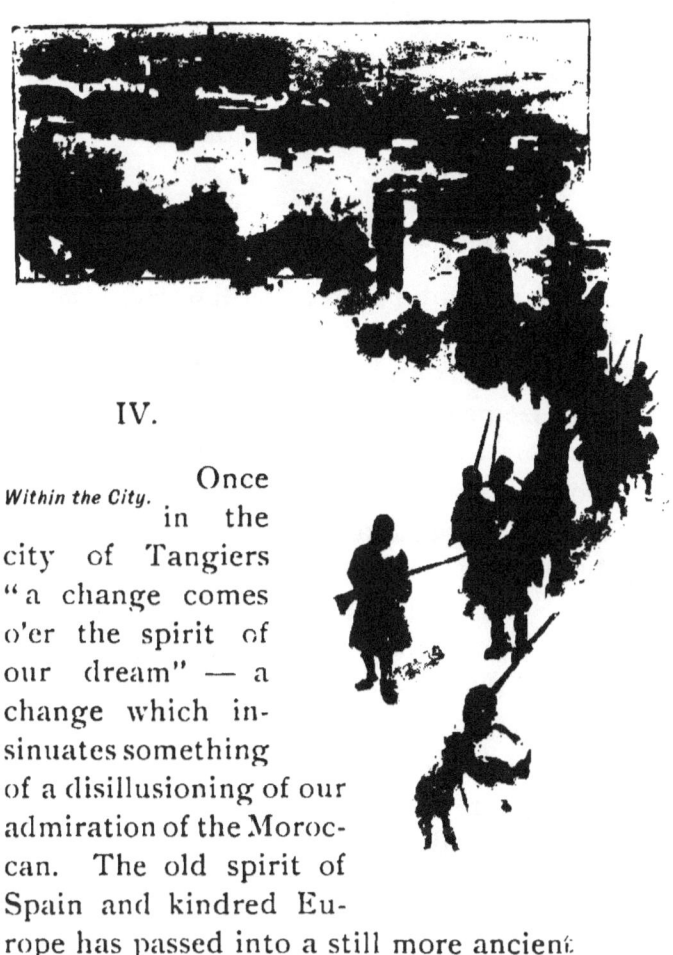

IV.

Within the City. Once in the city of Tangiers "a change comes o'er the spirit of our dream" — a change which insinuates something of a disillusioning of our admiration of the Moroccan. The old spirit of Spain and kindred Europe has passed into a still more ancient quality. How changed is all the present

world from that which occupies the little blue strip of land beyond those waters that lie like a broad, blue river between Andalusia and the land of the cres-
cent! The onward march of secular affairs seems suddenly halted, and the past
has found a living expositor in the dark-
brown bournouse and the white turban.
The estranged look of the eye, the quiet
shuffle of the sandal along the stone flagging, the dull passing interest with
which strangers are regarded, the shrill
pipe of the religious fanatic at the road-
side, and the grim airs of the patriarch
who salutes us with a " God-will "—all
seems more and more demanding of the
moment, and proves how removed from,
and ignoring of, the great leaping activities of our country and time, is the living present in this land of the Sultan
and the Bey.

Not even the ungracious interloping
of foreign charlatanism, or the boisterous innuendoes of modern life in this reposeful world so full of character and
color, has deposed that which in every
country of the East is supreme, the spirit
of mysticism and the *noblesse* of the con-

servative Moslem. We see French floun-
ces, English cork hats and American
slouch-caps intermixed in incongruous
promiscuity with the very crowds of
turbans and veils which lend such character and color to the neutral tints of
white-washed walls and opaque sky, and
drown effectively our own inartistic pres-
ences. What a creature of pure and unassimilating nature is the Arab! Bare
arms of light bronze thrust out of the
folds of a sombre bournouse, cheeks
thin and Cassius-like in their hungry
look, eyes sleepy and perfect in token of
the mysticism of his race, except when
intensely roused to action, and then
fierce and dancing, like two leaping
flames in the depth of the bronze twilight. His very walk betokens the child of
the wilderness, his very bearing mid these
low burnished walls like that of a captive who hates the confines of the village
and longs to return to the place of wider
latitude and more complete existence.
In the city, the Arab is but a fragment of
his free and native self under the blazing
sun, mounted on horse and scanning a
far horizon for the fear that his domin-

ion be invaded. How splendid in solitude, how ignoble in the crowd! The
prevalent odor of the Bedouin en-

camped in the outskirts, the camels
kneeling about upon the scanty pastur-
age, the little knots of women and children singing in shrill falsettos the song
of their early fathers, the quiet that al-
ternates the confusion of tongues when

the head of a family comes and goes, all seems to betoken captivity, yet it is that thought which perhaps the freest tribe of the wilderness would inspire.

The Native as he is. The Arab is a creature of wildest Utopianism, of the most fertile ingenuity with regard to effect in color, in language and in the *finesse* of war. He rides his inspired horse through all the realms of airy abstraction for the sole delight of the dream, not once looking to the value of the grand finale. The end of a great dream with him is seldom the beginning of a great deed. Begotten of a barbaric race of which women held all the vitalities of character and represented the higher values of the people, there is more of the woman in the man than he would lead us to suppose. The most manly men are those who admire, respect, and endeavor to broaden the influence of women, and who outwardly, as well as secretly, crave their society. The man who professes to ignore women, yet whose intense affinities with them demands polygamy and a harem, rather than monogamy and a home, is too much of the woman to allow dispute. Such an one has all the faults, and but few of the virtues, of his mother. It is everywhere glaringly evident, this constant ignoring of the influence of women upon the whole social regime of the East, but it is confessedly the menial position of woman, as a national factor, that accounts for the social organization, or, better, disorganization, of the race. As soon as woman is emancipated, the nation breaks the bonds that wrap it in its swaddling clothes. The Arab is too much of a woman, however splendidly his outward bearing belies him, ever to give women their freedom ; ever to admit that he loves, respects and cherishes them for their justice, their judgment and innate nobility. We, out of no strained effort to play the gallant, accord good women the highest places of national honor ; honor nobler than State or Church can give them. We recognize the fact that their intuitions are keener, less blunted by the ignoble contact of the hard, passionless business world ;

that, consequently, they are more honest and more reliable in times of extreme peril. The harshest judges are former criminals; the most brutal police, those who have themselves felt the club. Thus is it that when we find one who hates things womanly as much as a Moslem, yet who keeps a gorgeous harem secret from the eyes of the world, he has too much of his mother's faults and too few of her virtues ever to assume the title of superior manhood. Upon this theory is built, practically, all the weaknesses of a race. The child that abuses its younger and less rugged mates, is itself the victim of parental abuse. The reformed drunkard knows no tolerance of the drunkard unreformed; the man unforgiven, the last to forgive. We can readily account for the beggarly, measly, unheroic condition of the people of the Levant and India by the unmanly disrespect in which they hold their women, even as we may judge of their fortunate conquerors by their esteem of them, and their proven reliance in womanly intuitions when in times of extreme peril the man falters.

Moslem Social and Religious Law.   In most serene complacency, the Arab works out
his traditional scheme of spiritual econ-
omy. The Moslem is religious for a
greater reason, and, at the same time, a
less reason than reason itself—is a natural
hater of any other than his own system,
abhoring above all things the question-
ing of preconceived and pre-established
convictions.   While western Europe is
sleepless in the broil of solving· ethical
and spiritual problems by the aid of a
sort of rule-of-three science ; while
America is agitated to the core by the
invasion of French fatalism on the one
hand and esoteric mysticism on the other;
while Italy holds the infallible Pope a
prisoner, and the Archbishop of the
Greek Church of Russia endeavors to
reconcile the Slav spirit of freedom with
the Christ of the state religion, the Moslem sits regardless, heeding nothing of
the current perturbations that shake to
the roots the stunted growth of religious
fervor in other lands.   Superior to reason, in that to him one inspired word is

worth ten thousand deductions of science, he is ever beneath reason in that he tolerates no inspiration from sources other than his own. But if he is a fanatic without science or art to endue with an attractive grace the worship of his fathers, he has the rare power of abandoning himself to the spirit of his religion beyond all others. It would soon prove the depth of our religious fervor to exact of children and men the severe interest of the Mahommedan. Build a minaret in Soho or in Madison Square, and from the top of it let one of the more devout clergy call all hearers to prayer ; he would be regarded with amusement, and finally with contempt. Yet the Moslem in the midst of a business transaction will suddenly cut matters short at the cry of the muezzin in the distance—a cry which is to his trained ear as the cry of a babe to the ear of the mother—and, laying aside his outer garments, he prostrates himself toward Mecca, eyes dilate and far-estranged, non-present in the spirit, enwrapped in the most ecstatic religious trance. No king so preoccupied or majestic, no business man so absorbed in

his commercial struggles, no child so en-
grossed in his play that he hears not the
voice, and, what is more, heeds it.

The Slave Markets.   Slavery still exists in
Morocco, but the slaves'
power of attaining liberty is not impossible, and as they are distinguished
by fidelity and zeal for their masters,
superior rank is accorded them.   They
may possibly enter the ranks of the
body-guard, or swell the retinue of the
Sultan's court.   Slaves are generally
brought from the interior of Soudan
in childhood, and bred in the families of their owners.   Much has been
written and much excess of sympathy
has been wasted upon these unfortunates
whose greatest misfortune oftentimes is
to buy their freedom.   It is undeniably
a fact that the slave in the Moroccan
family, with plenty to eat, little to do,
good substantial clothes and treated
almost on equality with the children of
the household, is in a much more enviable position than the starveling sav-

age in the forests of Soudan. Though
no sensible nor humane man would ad-
vocate slavery, however it be counten-

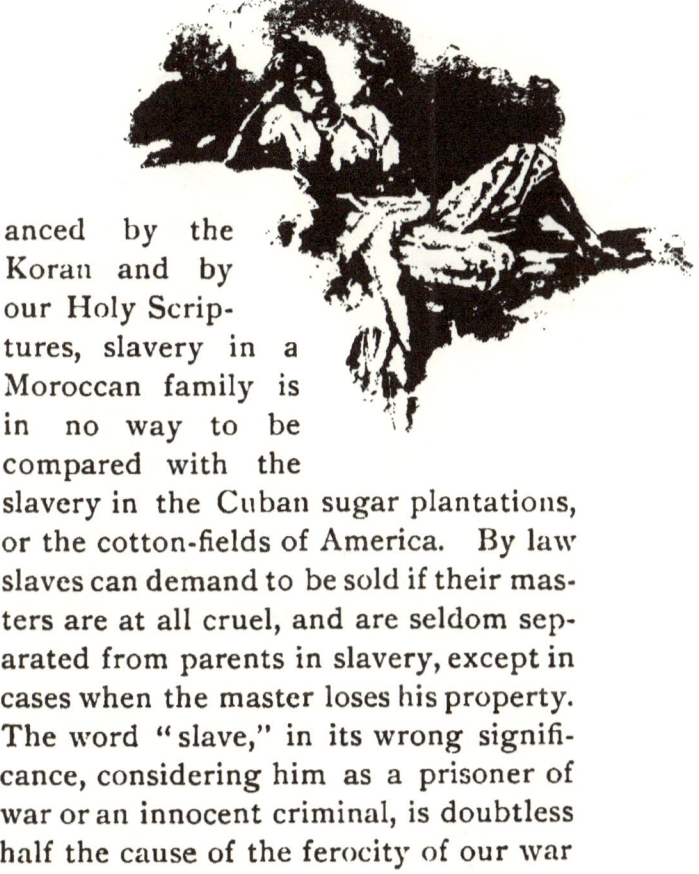

anced by the
Koran and by
our Holy Scrip-
tures, slavery in a
Moroccan family is
in no way to be
compared with the
slavery in the Cuban sugar plantations,
or the cotton-fields of America. By law
slaves can demand to be sold if their masters are at all cruel, and are seldom sep-
arated from parents in slavery, except in
cases when the master loses his property.
The word "slave," in its wrong significance, considering him as a prisoner of
war or an innocent criminal, is doubtless
half the cause of the ferocity of our war

of the rebellion. Here there is no direct
servitude; the slave is more of an attend-
ant—a servant, or apprentice ; more in
the light of a young man bound out to
learn a trade in England to-day. Were
the slaves of Morocco liberated, nine-
tenths would not leave the houses of
their masters, and the majority of the
freedmen would certainly starve. Still,
as may be imagined, the primitive system has many serious and pathetic
pictures, one of the most spirited and
vivid that we have ever read being from
the pen of Pierre Loti in his lately trans-
lated publication, "Into Morocco," the
verve and charming grace of the author
being admirably retained in the trans-
lation :—

"This evening, accompanied by my
usual companion, Captain H. de V.,
both of us dressed as Arabs, I took my
way to the slave market. The desolate
courtyard was untenanted. To our inquiry as to whether there would be any
business done this evening (for it is generally at nightfall, after the hour of the
Moghreb, that the slaves and the buyers
and sellers resort to this place), the an-

swer was returned : "We do not know; *but there is still that negro woman in the corner there, who is for sale.*"

" The negress was seated at the edge of one of those recesses which are excavated in the thickness of the old walls, like dens of animals; her attitude was one of great dread and terror, her head, enveloped in its grayish veil, and her closely covered face falling forward upon her breast; as she saw us upproaching, fearful, no doubt, that we were coming to buy her, she seemed to try to make herself smaller still. We made her arise so that we might look at her, as it is the custom to do with this kind of merchandise. We found that she was a little girl, sixteen to eighteen years old, whose tearful eyes bore an expression of resignation in the midst of a limitless despair; she was twisting her veil in her hands and kept her eyes directed toward the ground. What a pitiful sight it was, this poor little creature, who had meekly arisen to allow us to examine her, and who was awaiting her fate in this gloomy place. Beside her, seated in the same recess, was an elderly lady, her face

carefully concealed in her veil, who, notwithstanding her unpretending dress,
was evidently of the upper class. This
was the mistress, who had brought the
girl here for sale. We enquired the price;
five hundred francs. And the poor old
lady, with tears in her eyes and an expression almost as sad as that of her
slave, explained to us how she had
bought the child when very young and
brought her up, but that now, being re-
duced to poverty by the death of her
husband, she could no longer support
her and was obliged to part with her.
And thus it was that the two women
were here waiting to find a purchaser,
with a shrinking, humiliated air, both
equally disconsolate. It was like a mother
offering her daughter for sale."

But more reprehensible in the eyes of
the foreigner is the proverbial, ubiquitous wife-beater, who, be he Arab or Jew,
is sure to bring down the aspersion of
the Christian, who loves and reverences
the sex, upon his head with certain pre-
cipitation. While here in the city of
Tangiers there was great excitement on
account of the arrest and public whip-

ping of a Jew wife-beater, by our Consul,
Mr. Lewis. The wife had gone to the
Consul and complained a number of
times, and with her black and blue
bruises and welts has enlisted the Consul's sympathy, perhaps a little fur'her
than diplomatic policy justified. At any
rate, repeating the offense, the Jew was
lashed, deservedly, no doubt ; but it was
the occasion of a serious outbreak
amongst the Jews, who demanded the
recall of Mr. Lewis. Secretary of State
Blaine severely reprimanded the Consul
for taking the law into his own hands and
the result, hastened by numerous other
disagreements between the Consul and
his constituents, has occasioned his recall.

The Country Life. Nothing gave me quite
the swell of rapture that
the great valleys of wild flowers of Morocco inspired. Such a luxury is it to go
out into the fields and find the measure-
less waste now gay as a vast garden and
of infinite variety. Violet, iris and wild
geranium of a peculiarly hardy variety,

gladiolus, crimson as blood, and daffodils, all to me more beautiful in their native wildness than those which care and rich science had helped to be beautiful at home. Out beyond the cities the rich plains seem uninhabited quite save by the birds and flowers, and what contentment does not this rich solitude bespeak! I have always been friends with the lovers of flowers. Like the poet who fears the man that has no music in his soul, and as a child drawn to those who, it feels, will be kind and indulgent, so do I delight in the flower-lover, and lose no opportunity in proving my belief in his personal honesty and nobility of character. So, too, do we return to nature, and through one of her infinite lenses read the human heart, interpreting more reverently, more truly.

Art.   I do not wonder that the Arab's sense of color is so distinguished, though to the absolute disregard of all theories of form. His taste runs to the decorative rather than

pictorial art ; to carpets, rich, warm and
full of sympathy in color, like their own
variegated plains and valleys, and to arabesques—those nameless, varied and
concrete abstractions, which are rarely
heroic or dignified, yet always decorative, and to illuminations on the margins
of the Sacred Chronicles in the manner
of the Anglican monks.

Villages. The Moorish villages,
although distinct in char-
acter from those of the people further
east, are unvaryingly upon the same
fixed plans of site and arrangement. See
one, you see all. The unit is the exact prototype of ten thousand, and visiting any other of this number, can find
the same trades and shops upon the re-
lative spots ; at least, this was marvelously convincing to me, be it but an illusion. That square, monotonous mud hut,
thatched with reeds and protected from
nightly invasion by huge, ugly hedges
of the blue cactus, the tiny high windows, the open door, the rough carpet

at the threshold, and the noisy whistling storks on every roof—democracy with all its picturesque intensity, but dispiriting monotony. The greater number of these interior villages are the homes and haunts of thieves by religion—magnificent fellows, in whom the fine arts of villainy have reached a cultivated climax. The male members of the household are generally out on the forage, while the female members, guarded by a few straggling village parasites, remain to protect the scanty huts and their miserable, half naked young tigers of the desert, who so soon follow in the footsteps of the father. There is a certain dignity in the presence of these mounted marauders, men of the desert, who pillage caravans and overturn whole tribal empires now and then. They stand in their stirrups like bronze images of chivalry, flowing head-dress and mien of severe certainty of purpose, fleet, agile, invincible, splendid cowards. Like all barbarians, they hate the sight of civilization or any hinting thereto, save when the opportunity presents itself for plundering some straggling representative of it. Even the Sultan of Morocco is completely the tool, by fear, of some of these interior tribes, and never ventures his ambassadors, to say nothing of his own precious person, in their midst.

To us, who have known every species of outlaw, from the Missouri guerilla to the Sierra Nevada stage-robber, these splendid pirates of the desert bear something of the heroic and chivalrous withal, and the fierce, tigerish manner of capturing their prey, leads us to somewhat soften the rigor of our judgment in their favor. Men despise the sneak, the crawling, cringing, snake-like dastard who watches the victim's departure to rob him of that which he has left unguarded ; but there is such a thing as a dignity of villainy, which, even if we are not bound to respect, we can consider with softened consciences. It must not be forgotten in extenuation of the Arab outlaw, that it is his heredity, his breeding, his very religion, to crush his natural enemies: the usurper of his lands and the subverter of his faith. The North American Indian has all the justifications of self-defense on the former score—that of pro-

tecting his hunting-grounds from mercenary invaders, who are no respecters of the property of those not their equal in war—but the Indian has not this great natural force beneath and beyond all thought of material gain : a fanatical religion, to make him fierce and vindictive. The cold, barbaric heroism upon which Cooper founds his plots of American nomad life, and which lends such verve and interest to Hiawatha and the legion of Indian heroics, is not to be compared with this vast unwritten series of legends of the plains beyond the belts of civilization in Morocco, where the barbarian is still in power, defenseless in a way, yet personally invincible, with all consciousness of high duty in murdering to save his own, and, above all, to apotheosize his whole family, by dipping his hands in the blood of a giaour. Of all wars, the religious war is the most spirited, abandoned, heathenish. Each cries to God, believing that the one all-seeing Eye is upon him, and him alone.

Language.   Corrupted by the successive innovations of for-
eign idiom and trade colloquialism, the
early purity of the language, since the
time of Ibu Khaldum, like the tongues
of all the Orient, has passed out of its
condition of purity, and remains only a
thread of gold, as it were, running
through a conglomerate fabric of dia-
lects. Philology is a most dispiriting
study in this land of linguistic dissipa-
tion, where there is really so little held
in the rigid bounds of philological law,
and so much the accidental and the arbitrary. The dispersion of the Jews in
their own lands, and their scattering set-
tlements along the north coast of Africa
and forthwith assuming the monetary
dominion of the country invaded, has
been much the cause of the decadence
of the pure, natural Arab language,
while the successive, and not unoften
successful Spanish invasions of later
centuries, have left a perceptible Spanish
infusion of idiom in the current coin of

the tongue. This accounts for the diversity of religious opinion, even in the most fanatical ranks, and also in a measure accounts for the poverty of anything bordering upon an established literature.

Church and State. The present condition of Morocco, considered politically, could hardly be worse. The quasi-hereditary Sultan is a despot supreme, having power of life and death over his subjects at any and all times— in war, or peace; in times of religious fanaticism, and in times of religious apathy. The meting out of justice is most arbitrary, and the administrative functionaries of the State attend to their duties with appalling laxity and with extreme inconsistency at times. The punishment of criminals is, as a rule, most shockingly cruel, recalling the mediæval barbarities of the early church which inherited that certain quality of inflicting pain without conscience or mercy, from the persecutions of its own adherents

by the Romans. The feudal doctrine of
the North, which happily has passed
away, has here an expositor on every
tract, and the very shepherd and plow-
man carries a weapon of self-defense
slung across his shoulders. The army,
most inadequate, unreliable and ill-paid,
the navy, rotting in the harbors of Carash,
slavery in full license, country roadless,
untraversable save by camel or horse
single file, no bridges, no inns, and the
danger of travel for even the Sultan beyond the nearest borders to civilization
—all this, as may readily be conjectured,
conspires to keep Morocco in the dark
ages, and, if possible, plunge her into
more direful ignominy.

Comparisons.   That this fertile, beautiful region should be
called the China of the West, is prepos-
terous indeed, for two reasons: first, that
in no manner, either with regard to climate, or to topographical position of
country, or fertility of soil, does it resem-

ble China, or in any way does the high
state of civilization in some parts of
China resemble the barbarism here.
There is no native civilization here, while
there is in China. The civilization that
skirts the borders of the Mediterranean
is the reflection—an infusion of the civilization of Europe. It is not native, it is
not indigenous. That Morocco is infested
with tribal factions which, as long as
they hold control of the most valuable
portions of the country, will keep the
people in abject barbarism, is most true;
that there exists anything of this state
of affairs in China, is not true. To re-
proach China with being the Morocco
of the East, would be stigmatizing the
former most brutally. To call Morocco
the China of the West, is senseless flat-
tery.

The land of the iris and daffodil,
where great valleys and mountain passes
are filled with marigold and heather,
one may naturally expect to find rich in
fruits. No country of the world could
yield such fruits, were it only under
proper cultivation. As it is, heavy ex-
ports of figs from Fez and other interior

towns, famous oranges from Tetuan, pomegranates from Morocco, and dates from Akka, besides almonds and olives from divers provinces, attest the fact, that with so much of nature on their side, such a people could accomplish the marvels in horticulture that were achieved in the reign of Abderrahman of Spain.

One thing that shows remarkable barbarian sagacity is the underground graneries, which everywhere are to be seen in the country. These graneries hold vast amounts of grain often, and preserve it in good condition for years. They resembled, in my mind, the dugouts of Nebraska, where a man cuts a hole in the hillside and runs his chimney up grotesquely to the top of the hill, satisfied with the light and ventilation afforded by a door, and a window over it. I have also seen cellars in the West for the purpose of shelter in case of the approach of cyclones, when there is danger of the high winds of the blizzard blowing down the frail frame house. Of these, too, the Arab underground graneries—one of the best feats of barbarian engineering, by the way, which I have been privileged to compliment the race upon—reminded me forcibly.

I have used the terms Moor and Arab controvertably, for, although there is a distinction, and a strong one, it is rather a distinction resulting from contact with civilized life, rather than a distinction of race. The Moors, of course, mainly occupying the cities on the coast, are considered the superior people, and from his preferring a home to a tent, which the Arab does not, he assumes his nobility. The Berber, doubtless the descendant of the aboriginal races, is the mountaineer, who occupies a social position distinct from either the Moor in the city, or Arab on the plains and in the valleys beneath them. The Berber builds houses of clay, and sometimes substantially of stone. Doubtless, what really native civilization the inhabitants of Morocco can boast, the Berbers possess and will retain. They are conservative and industrious, and being of a hardier clime— the difference between the highlands and the plains being so great as to produce a distinct race of people—take the value for the little heroism the country affords, be it the heroism of defensive warfare, or the ferocity of the outlaw.

Algeria

VII.

" And when thou enterest thy tent, let every evil retire ;
praise God and the Prophet, and prosperity be
thy lot."—*From a Bedouin Poem.*

" A good traveler will not be blind to a people's good
qualities, and only point the finger at defects."
—*An Arab Adage.*

I.

Off for New Scenes. We left Tangiers by Steamer "Malverna,"stopping for a short time at the ports of Gibraltar, Malaga and Malilla—the latter place a well-fortified Spanish town which is the prison city of the kingdom. Nemours, the first French town that we stopped at in Algeria, is a strongly fortified military seaport, and again we meet the trim attire and dignified bearing of the French infantry officer. Oran, the next Algerian city visited, is of some considerable size and commercial importance, being the nearest of these several ports to Spain, besides being a picturesque study from the sea as well as an exceedingly rich repository of legend and antiquity. In contemplating the fierce period of war under Ferdinand cf Spain and the later overthrow by the French, this little town occupies a position of no small importance. Its sheltered location offers a favorable port of refuge for ships that are caught in the sudden and treacherous white squalls of the Mediterranean, and the healthful and vigorous condition of the natives attest the fact that it thrives as much by adverse winds as by the calm of prosperity. The city rises like a Roman amphitheatre from the calm waters, the larger portion resting upon the two wide plateaux divided by a ravine, deep, shady and most enchantingly picturesque. The houses are corniced in the Morisco style, with flat, terraced roofs, and colored awnings and curtains to relieve the quiet monotony. The ravine that divides the city is the home of the foreign population, as might be inferred, and is beautified with a series of most enchanting gardens. Through it a stream flows, on its flanks the pale green of the plantain-tree standing bold against the riper contrasting tints of the pomegranate and citron.

The Caravan. At Oran we took the train for the city of Algiers, and were delighted with the comforts afforded by a palace car, small, but with seats at the sides, leaving a roomy space in the center. One of the first pleasures on leaving the city was to pass very near a caravan of camels coming into Oran from the southeast, loaded with various products of the fertile plateaux beyond. There is a somewhat indefinably inspiring in the sight of these great, moving repositories of commerce, legend and oriental character, which strikes the beholder fresh from a world of steam and telegraph, with a sense of repose and calmness truly pleasing. The camel, most picturesque and patient of all burden-bearing animals, gives a quality to all he bears, and to all his surroundings. Transport him to Poland, and his Polish keeper is suddenly transformed into an Arab, and all the dull avenues of a conventional northern life, become tropic and replete with qualities of vigor and color. Without his camel, what an unsightly pirate has the Arab

become—out of his sphere, like an un-
horsed jockey, with cap, and whip, and
stirrup,—all that which dignifies the
man, severely wanting.   The instant the

camel is at his side, the picture becomes
complete; and what was dead and color-
less is now animated and interesting.

After all, our machines for quick
transportation and labor-saving convenience are most characterless.   Mechan-

ism awes us, but inspires the interest of the intellect at the expense of the affections. Faithful dogs, wise and noble horses and camels, quicken our admiration, and not unoften inspire our genuine love. Now, surely, that which so fervently quickens our love, has the power of begetting true character—nobility. The day approaches when cables and dynamos supersede horses, and railways, the camel, even as guns have superseded the cross-bow and the falcon, and the telegraph the carrier-pigeon. But by a law of compensation, what we gain in speed and mere material convenience, we lose in that indefinable, yet inestimable quality, called character. Fast living and slow thinking—and what true thought but is profoundly deliberate—never go hand-in-hand. The caravan is an open history; a living illustration of a dead legend, a forgotten era. It will soon pass away, and, though more convenient burden-bearers will take the place of it, the character that gives it its distinguishable charm, will fade away with it, and nothing so inspiring of our reverence take its place.

An Incident. Soon again we pass down the valley of the river Chelif, the low river-bottom brown and parched under the fierce tropic sun. The Arabs are cutting grain, and we pass through a large section where the rye is standing in stacks, one of which has taken fire, perhaps from the sparks of our locomotive. From all directions, on foot, on horse and camel-back, the poor natives are flocking to the rescue, and with blankets and flails begin the almost futile fight with the destroyer of their whole year's labors. It is but a momentary scene of excitement and peril, and as if ignoring the sufferings of those we leave behind, we plunge up the valley and cut into the heart of the mountains.

The Country. The fertile lowlands through which we have passed, now so hard and parched, in the Spring and Winter are spread out like a series of gardens of richest verdure and bloom. The only relief of the hard steeps and the fierce sky, is the dotting here and there of Moormen's tents and huts, and the white cottages of the foreigner that cluster about the mineral springs on the mountain eminence beyond. From the desert vales of the river Chelif, out of this region of dry and parching summer, we pass into an atmosphere of Spring, the rich verdure on every hand attesting the fact that even a small country like Algeria, has the advantages of a diversity of climate. As we emerge from noisy tunnels, new views of beauty and interest greet us, and until night closes in and the sunset grows sombre and vague ; we watch the changing scenes, and then with the two Moors who have joined us in our snug cabin, and who by their dress and general bearing indicate all the refinements of their strange race, we take our sleep until we arrive at the city of Algiers.

II.

The windows of our rooms in this snug and *Algiers.* scrupulously clean hotel—*de la Oasis*—command a fine view of the bay, upon whose clear, beautiful waters numerous French and foreign ships and contrasting barques of oriental hull and sail, move lazily about or lie sleeping at anchor. We took an early walk through the business part of the city which looks bright and attractive, the bazaars and shops inviting and full of interest to the searcher after the picturesque and the characteristic. It is Saturday, and con-

sequently the Jews have closed their
shops, leaving the dupeable public to
the less tender mercies of the Mahommedan and the Christian. In Algiers, quite
contrary to the ancient rhyme, three
Sundays come together. Friday the
Mahommedans, Saturday the Jews, and
Sunday the Christians, celebrate their
Sabbath. Later in the morning we enjoyed a carriage ride into the country,
taking the winding road that leads up
the steep hill-side, the palaces and less
pretentious homes looking like terraced
streets from above. The city reminded
me from the first of Genoa on the bay
of Spezzia, the coloring, perhaps, a little
richer in depth and feeling. The view
from the summit of the hill behind the
city is inspiring indeed; the bright blue
bay beneath and beyond, flocked with
queerest barques and gorgeous sails like
skimming butterflies touching lightly the
brim of the sea, to the south, the Moorish
palaces, fantastic and enchanting, the
French villas dotting the hillside, and
here and there a green vineyard flanked
by hedges of cacti and blossoming wil-
low, and yonder a high kiosk of some

dignitary's harem, and on either side the bright dome of the Mahommedan place of worship.

The Trappists. We were driven out over the plateau beyond the hill, which so benignantly overlooks the city, and came upon a remarkably well cultivated section, well fenced, and with every indication of prosperity and thrift, and learn that it is the property of a colony of religious anchorites, called the Trappists, who were granted this tract of twenty-five hundred acres, which they have transformed from a desert wilderness into a most luxuriant garden. Orange, olive, apricot trees in profusion, thrifty and attended with all the science of careful horticulture, stand on our left, while vegetables and flower-gardens of every variety sweep down the valley to our right as we pass up toward the monastery. Here we are met by the most hospitable of men—an old monk, with a strong, characteristic face, and the manners of a nobleman. After all, the conservatism of even an Algerian monk be-

gets a certain repose of manner and dignity of presence, which the cosmopolite,
whose manners are moulded by the force
of ever-changing contact, can but admire.   The long, brown, woollen robe of
the order, the snowy white hair, the san-
daled feet, and the great bunch of keys
hanging at the belt—all this seems to
give a nobleness to the hospitality so
generously extended us, and we feel a
pleasure in bestowing reverence upon
this calm despiser of the world which we
ourselves so deeply and constantly enjoy.

" You must not come with us," said the
venerable Trappist to a lady who had
accompanied us hither, a bow of profoundest apology mitigating the rigor
of his command, " for none but men are
admitted into the inner court."   Then,
with expressions of regret to the disap-
pointed one, we were ushered through
the great stone corridors, so silent and
cold, and were shown the monastery from
turret to foundation-stone—from gran-
ery to the huge wine-cellar.   From well-
filled barns and sheds, which indicate
such commendable thrift, out to the machine shops, we passed, and at the latter

place were surprised to find an Ohio threshing machine at work by the side of an ancient stone grinding-mill which might have been handed down from the graneries of Solomon. The little chapel was of all other solemn places in this place of perpetual worship, the most dismal, and to me, seemingly the least inviting of religious enthusiasm; but the sight of the careworn, pale and emaciated features of the monks who knelt about and chanted their doleful *Miserere*, was surely most impressive. The fact that the monks are never allowed to speak to one another upon the passing events, and that there are other equally inflexible rules which increase the hardship of the severely plain surroundings, the Trappist's life is assuredly not a happy one. They are allowed to salute one another at morning, however, with the chilling phrase, "Good morrow, brother, remember that we must die!" crossing the hands upon the breast with the solemn greeting. Their bed-rooms resemble cells in the severest aspect of prison life. Small, bare, with beds so narrow and hard, surely very little com-

fort is enjoyed even there. The dining
room is furnished quite as uninviting to
the appetite as the bed-room is to the
tired body. Bare tables, long black
benches, and a crust at each place, is the
banquet hall and the repast ; and while
even this intensely frugal meal is being
enjoyed, a brother in the pulpit at the
end of the room reads prayer after
prayer in the most maddening monotone, which doubtless adds dryness to
the crust.

All this is in unwholesome contrast to
the rich gardens of flowers which skirt
the dismal monastery, and the wide
groves of orange, lemon and citron
which flank the south wings. Our admiration for their genial hospitalities to
strangers was again renewed with their
spreading before us a refreshment which
was truly luxurious, even if it was far
more worldly than the spiritual repast
we refrained from partaking in company
with the anchors within the grim dining
hall. Fine white bread, cakes, and two
kinds of wine of their own successful,
and, indeed, famous make—these most
unmonkish refections, together with de-

licious large strawberries, and apricots fresh from the boughs, were our boun-ties, of which, fortunately for her, the lady who accompanied us hither, was permitted to partake. One old monk, who particularly interested us, and who plied us with all conceivable questions, relating to the outer world which, though he so despised, he was willing to hear about, surprised me by taking down a map of the United States and telling us of a colony of the Trappist order in Louisville, Kentucky, and also of one in Iowa. These facts brought the vener-able body into a somewhat nearer focus, as it were, and was the occasion of not a little interchange of compliment. The lady remarked with a delicate shrewdness : " Generally the monks whom I have visited in Greece and else-where seem to be very contented and happy in their several monasteries; but here they all look so sad. Are they not happy then ? "

" Why should they not be happy, serv-ing God so faithfully ? " was his sagac-ious counter-question.

The monks who showed us these particular favors, and who were doubtless deputized to entertain strangers, seemed to want to hold fast to us till the last moment, and learn of the outside world. The reason was that they are only allowed to talk to strangers, hence their anxiety to retain them to break the long and certainly most stupid monotony of their rigorous anchorage. Even our American watches interested them greatly, and the merest trifles of our conventional apparel and manners were objects of scrutiny and interest to them. Here we found the famous motto: *"S' il est triste de vivre à la Trappe qu' il est doux d'y mourir."*—If this be a hard place to live, it is a good place to die?

The order was founded in the twelfth century, by Rotron Comte de Perche, who built the first monastery of the order in the department of Orme in France. In 1845, the French government granted the Trappists this land, then the desert hiding-lairs of the wild boar and the tiger, and from a wilderness of brushwood and palmetto, they have changed it into a garden of rare beauty and prosperity.

Street Scenes. The grand city promenade passes in front of our Hotel l'Oasis. It is the " Boulevard de la Republique," and runs along the sea, overlooking the broad and busy harbor some four thousand feet. In the evening this attractive breathing space is populous with a curious crowd of French, Arabs, Moors and Jews, the latter three seemingly glad to receive an hour of immunity from the prison slavery of the dark inner alley-ways of the thronged and silent city. The Jews are a particularly interesting feature of Western oriental life. Somehow this ubiquitous, irrepressible child of Israel seems to thrive on the insults and inhumanities of barbarian tribe and civilized race alike. The warm, tropic sun and the dull sirocco have moulded these other tribes of the Semetic race into a distinct type, although the characteristic features to be met with in Palestine, Poland and Mulberry Street, are preserved irradicably ; the aquiline nose, small, keen, brilliant eye, clear, almost pallid complexion, and beard of formal cut, black as night. Stooping under the weight of oppression that is never lifted, severe intent upon making up in the viles of business the social stigma he has borne for ages, quarreling, snarling, dogged, acquisitive, here as everywhere else, they manage to encircle the whole commercial regime. Active, quick-witted, versatile, all inroads into the heart of trade are commanded by them, and with the semblance of enjoying life, are in reality the most miserable of peoples.

The Women. The Jewish women do not cover the face with veils, and the striking beauty of the younger matrons and maidens is a redeeming feature of the noisy, dirty Jews' quarter. The artistic *sarmah*—very like the ancient Biblical *hennin*—the full gown unconfined at the waist, short sleeves, bare feet, and beautiful hair which in the younger members of the family is allowed to fall unbound over their shoulders, the feminine half of the Algerian Jew is interesting and fair. The Turks, who were their rulers before the

French entered upon the stage, were harsh, cruel and merciless. Hence, the  Israelites hailed the advent of the French with delight, and in consequence, have turned the tables on the Ishmaelites, whom they treat with the cruelty oftentimes that they themselves experienced at the hands of the Mahommedan.

The Cathedral. On Sunday morning we went to the famous Cathedral of the Black Virgin, or *Notre Dame d'Afrique* where a Bishop was to receive consecration, and where, consequently, we found standing-room at a premium. The pontifical robes were gorgeous indeed. We noted above the

altar the famous Black Virgin, and this
inscription, "Our Lady d'Afrique prays
for us and for all poor Mussulmans." The
church occupies a striking eminence on
a spur of the Mount Bou-Zarea, and
commands an extraordinary breadth of
view : the great city, the sea, and the far
mountains of Djurdjura. It is Byzan-
tine in style, with high central dome
lifting from a cluster of smaller ones,
and flanked by a tall minaret, reminding
me much of the Greek church in Fin-
land. As this is peculiarly the sailor's
church, votive offerings in most incongruous profusion, hang about the walls ;
small ships, crutches, war arms, legs,
eyes, and other freaks attesting the mi-
raculous restoration of these members in
the superstitious votaries of this black
patroness, and every Sunday afternoon
the impressive ceremony for the repose
of those buried at sea takes place at the
edge of the cliff overlooking the Mediterranean.

III.

The Native Quarters. We passed through the Arab quarter on our return, visiting the more famous of the mosques. At Tangiers, we were not permitted to visit the Mahommedan place of worship, and the giaour who undertook to pass the threshold, would have done so at his extreme peril. But here, by taking off our shoes and retaining our hats, both in token of respect, we enter the court where a picturesque group of Moors are bathing at the marble fountain, and, their ablutions done, we follow them as they pass into the great mosque. There, lifting their hands, they prostrate themselves in profoundest humility, face toward the East, eyes dilate and almost closed in the ecstasy of divine revealment, lips uttering passage after passage of the Koran, punctuated by repetitions of the humble obeisance to the " Allah who is good, and to Mahommet who is his prophet."

The Moslem's Devotion. The devotion of a Mahommedan to his religion furnishes a foreigner with a subject for contemplation. The laws of the church are very strict, and are adhered to with astonishing rigidity. There is a fascination in this ecstasy for most of the devotees, and nothing will induce a worshipper to neglect his devotions for an instant—not even the threat of death, or what is worse, the threat of losing the sale of a trinket to a European for twenty times its value. At home, it would, indeed, seem queer to punish a bad boy by keeping him home from church of a Sunday morning; yet this is the worst punishment inflicted by the Mahommedan father upon his refractory son.

The Bazaars. The old Arab quarter with its narrow, characteristic streets, shops invitingly decked, with overhanging balconies and fine lattice windows, is a place of great interest.

The principal avenue, narrow at best, ascends the hill step by step, and is a series of surprises. Here is a *tibeel*, or apothecary, with his little booth filled with  nostrums and roots concealed in quaint old jars and odd-shaped flasks, a little forge for heating red hot the irons with which they heroically puncture the flesh in rheumatic and pleuritic cases, boxes of knives for cupping—an ancient barbarity still in vogue — and other oddities of mediæval times. Here, also, in various receptacles of odd design, prickly pear leaves for bruises, ground pine for fevers, scabious for ague, birthwort for colic, alkermes for small-pox, and rows upon rows of little specifics which have received the sanction of domestic home-doctoring in the Moorish circle, and as a last resort, perhaps—alas ! how futile is

even science in times of peril—little boxes
of *magareah*, or amulets, which, when all
else has failed, will purge the infected
body and soul as by the touch of mir-
acle. There sits a lazy dreamer over
his box of childish trumpery, and at our
approach he waxes himself into a spirit
of aggression, till his brown robe falls
from his shoulders, exposing a withered,
tawny physique made proportionless
by the hardship of repose rather than
of severe labor. Beyond him, a pair of
fair Jewesses, leading picturesque little
urchins with pink complexions and tiny
sprouts of curls dangling before their
ears, the young damsels with narrow
eyebrows and waxen features, and a step
with all the stealth of a captive gazelle.
We pass another booth of a well-to-do
silk merchant, and catch a glimpse of
his favorite wife as she turns to glance
at us and then glides up the stone steps
out of sight, her rich dress, embroidered
sandals and profusion of jewels adorn·
ing her perfect limbs, attest her favor
with her lord. What a dignified bearing! What a look of content and ease!
Our friend, the guide, warns us to be-

ware of the sly, knowing glances of the
solemn Moor at the entrance of the
booth, assuring us that these savage
fellows are very jealous and revengeful.
Then we come upon a marble fountain
in the middle of a small court whose
enclosing walls are overhung with jas-
mine, ivy, and beautiful trailing vines,
in which enclosure a flock of impish
little urchins are playing noisily and
happily. A shower of pennies brings
them about us, and their bright, grotesque little faces and outstretched hands
make a series of pictures illustrating,
perhaps, the most interesting phrase of
Algerian life — the only really happy
period—that of childhood. Their musi-
cal trebles, like the chatter of so many
jackdaws, makes the language appear so
easy and natural that one is tempted to
take up the study of a literature at once
so simple, rich and resonant, and fitting
the lips with such felicity; but doubtless this illusion, like many another
Eastern paradox, vanishes upon closer
observation.

Algerian Women. This leads me to observe that of all slavery, that of the Algerian woman is not the least enviable —if one may be privileged to envy a slave in any condition or country. The better class of Moors and Arabs take pride in keeping their women carefully housed and fed, and incidents of cruelty to wives, with which the French courts

have of late so summarily dealt, all occur among the lower orders. Perhaps if cruelty did exist within these perfumed gardens and luxurious palaces of the native rich, no one without would

ever know of it ; but from the glimpses
of native life with which one is now and
then rewarded by glancing through an
open door, between curtains drawn aside
at the lattice, or by contemplating this
luxury from the low terraces, the women
seem to be immeasurably happy, the
care-worn, painful look of despair which
we see upon many refined faces at home,
never once greeting us. The veil over
the face is a happy invention, for the
eyes of the native Moor or Arab are the
most expressionful of the features, leaving to the imagination the picturing of
a beautiful mouth and pink cheeks behind the ruse which but conceals, probably, a degree of ugliness. The women
spend their pretty lives spinning, em-
broidering, and listening to the tales of
a hired story-teller—a female of vast resources, and generally better versed in
the intricacies of successful gossip than
in the legends of the Mahommedan
heroes.

V.

The Fatalism of the Moslem. The Arabs are, by their nature and breeding, fatalists, and hence we seldom see objects of stern solemnity treated with what, in the Occident, we would esteem true reverence. Even the dead, as may be seen by the indifferent manner in which they are borne away on the shoulders of the twelve pall-bearers, are not exempt from the chilling lack of interest with which the presence of momentous facts inspires men the world over. The cemeteries, so picturesque with their creeping vines, weeping willows, cypress and wild flowers, are places of repose for the soon forgotten. It is seldom the graves of the departed are revisited with a renewing of tears and recalling of tender memories. They are *dead*. That means, to the Arab, that they never lived. With the death of the wife, father, brother, the memory of each of them perishes. So cruelly cold are the majority of Arabs that not even in times of great peril, when buildings fall and people are imprisoned beneath the ruin, or a ship is foundering at sea, will the Arab risk his own life to save those of his own family.   Allah desired to call them to heaven for a purpose. Why should he interfere with the great God, and possibly incur His displeasure?

VI.

The French Colonization. The French occupation of Algiers and other north African countries, strikes the disinterested observer, foreign to both France and these countries, with a peculiar sense of the injustice of this sort of aggression. To a country with an overburdened population, wholesale land-grabbing holds something of an extenuating clause; but where there is land and law, wherein every one who wills can set up his household gods and not feel his neighbor crowding him, this splendid modern piracy is unchristian in a pitable extreme. The Dey Hussein slaps the face of the French consul-general—a wantonly familiar thing to happen even in a hut—and because it occurs in a palace, the French answer with cannon and shell. It is the old school-boy trick, when the booby has the apple which the bully wants, and justifies himself in forcing a quarrel to gain. It is well to argue the fact that, previous to French occupation, the country was infested with pirates and bandits, which

their presence has effectively extermin-
ated. But this only adds weight to the
fact that therein the French demon-
strate their own superior capabilities as
banditti. The French at home, however,
are acute and courageous in their judg-
ments, and none criticise the blunders
of French colonization with keener
scrutiny than do they themselves. But
it is a pretty, convenient fiction of law,
which has already become a reality, that
possession is nine-tenths of the yard stick
of justice wherewith we would mete the
disputed possession, and that twenty
years of occupation brings into convenient leverage a statute of limitations ;
hence, doubtless, it is well to yield the
point to the tenant, who once held in
trust for another, but now holds treasures
for his own.

Poverty. What strikes the heart
of the well-fed, warmly-
housed American, fresh from a land of
plenty and prosperity, is the overwhelming amount of misery that silently pleads
for succor at the hands of foreigners.
Silently, for the most deserving are in-

deed not the loudest in their prayers, though by far the sincerest in their gratitude. At all hours of the day I met on the outskirts of the city, poor, emaciated forms of cast-out humanity, like an old shoe that has outworn its usefulness, thrown into the great city's garret—the outskirts. If such is the misery in time of peace, what must it be in time of war, when even water is so precious, and when the scant supply of food is scantier still? Every day and even every hour of the day, it almost seems, my sympathies are called out, and a grovelling wretch with the grimy burnous about his shrunken shoulders, his hollow eyes and parched tongue, and voice like a judgment from the under world, staggers me with the keenness of this picture of misery, and the gratitude of his heart in response to my trifling benefactions almost haunts me with its fervency. Gorgeous sunsets over waters that sleep so placidly about the tropical peninsula, fair faces of young girls at the fountains, filling their *amphoræ* with water, and carrying them away again upon their white, round shoulders,

palaces and mosques that tempt the
eye and feast the sense to satiety—
all these gentle regalements continually
intermix with scenes of the most coarse
and abandoned realism, and prove that
even the advent of Christianity, and the
refinements of French civilized life, have
not eradicated the traces of a fallen, de-
graded, outcast people, whose holy
Prophet has done what little he could to
make fanatical and worthless the small
residuum of the primitive man who certainly was endowed with something that
begets prosperity—be it by labor of the
head or hand—else we ourselves should
not be a race to-day. Something must
be done to make the Arab and the Moor
self-supporting. There are thousands
of acres of arable land, yet no one
ventures to turn the soil. The Moor has
emulated the Jew whom he pretends to
despise—emulated him by attempting
to live by his wits as the child of Israel
does, yet not possessing the profound
subtilty in business caution that is the
very source of the Hebrew's success.
He leaves the farm for the jewelry-shop,
only to find that these trinkets can be

manufactured in Birmingham for less than they can make them ; and, consequently, another pauper rides the Jackhorse of Christian charity, which poor steed appears to be something of a spavined old jade here in Algeria.

VII.

Conservatism of the Moor. In the gradual but effectual desuetude of old and cherished rites and observances all about him, the Arab remains what Peacock would call a *Statue-quo-ite.* He is a child of the past, of barbaric fanaticism, with fervent religious veneration for anything and all that is force—a power temporal as well as spiritual. He is a splendid dreamer, whose dreams have flattered him with dominions which were rather a trust-fund than a real possession ; and he has seen the precious charge wantonly wrested from his grasp by a people whose religion he despises, whose morals he abhors, whose temporal force he covets. When from the principal avenues of the French quarter so bustling, modern, extraneous to

the land, and apparently to the times,
the observer turns up the alley that
leads like a pilgrim's stairway through
the dark, silent city of the Arab, he
plunges into a sepulchre, as it were—a
whited prison-tomb, gloomy, ghostly
without, and rich, resplendent, full of
ancient grace within.   But the whole is
a sealed book to him.   A door ajar, a
glimpse of the marble court, a lattice
aside, disclosing a divan whence its fair
occupant has just fled, and a pot of
flowers on a queer pedestal by the embroidered curtain: a glimpse here, the
merest inkling of the mystery there, and
the great enigma of Moslem life remains
unsolved.   Even while we stand in contemplation a moment in the early twilight, a queer figure darts out of a secret
door, passes along and fades away like a
spectre in the mazes of arched alleys and
impenetrable depths where all is life
and activity shrouded in utterest silence.
The short cry of a babe and hiss from
the mother's lips, as if it might betray
the secret hiding; the quick yelp of a
dog that would break the monotony
through fear; the rustle of the silken

robes of some passer-by who for but one
single instant is outlined against the
gloomy wall—these are the only sounds
to make merry the awful spell which
hangs like a curse upon the fallen city.
The great gulf between the past and the
present, between the Mahommet and
Christ, between the successful invader
and the fallen invaded, seems to lie
placid and calm at our feet, growing
ever wider and wider, till at last the few
sympathies that are left—and they, alas,
are only the affinities of vice—will
cease, and the Arab will merge into a
concrete type, having "suffered a sea-
change" as it were, into something less
of himself and more of him whose vices
now, and soon his virtues, he would
emulate.

VIII.

Political Life.   There is a cosmopoli-
tanism in these Moorish
diplomates and men of affairs which is
quite in contradistinction to the reserve
of these conservative people. There is
an undeniable dignity which the thin

white veils and the at best rude civili-
ties of Moslem genuflection will not dis-
guise, nor permit one to altogether lose
sight of in the study of events and the
personages that have their being in
them. The scholarly indolence which so
admirably gives character to the Moslem, is not wanting ; but he who has the
affairs of the market upon his mind, must
necessarily mix with men of other times
and of other temperaments, and receive
no inconsiderable infusion of their habits.
It seems at times strange that these
superb men of the desert—wild native
outcasts, so fanatical, so wild, could ever
stoop to the machinations of diplomatic
courtesies, and assume the intelligible
rôle of the high-binder in eminence.
But the thirst for wealth and influence
has broken down the conservatism of the
race, and schooled men in the corrup-
tions of political life, into which their
sons shift so ill-advisedly, embracing all
the intriguing vulgarities of politics,
with scarcely a redeeming drop of its
nobility,

Climate. It is with unalloyed pleasure that I note the varying atmospheric changes which are so sudden and impressive in these southern climes, so resplendent and magical in their display of variation. From my windows I look out upon the horizon, noting the thin blue threading of the coast of Europe along the brim of the opalescent waters which seem so varied in their play of hues; and watch, too, the masses of cloud, cheerless indeed would they appear by the cold northern peaks, but here now full of caprice, now indolent, and then chased away into nothingness to give place to the warm limpid depths of a southern sky, than which nothing is more enchanting. After leaving the turgid activities of Europe, the quiet and repose of this venerable city fills me with a certain passion which doubtless is somewhat akin to that love of introspection and ease which characterizes the types I constantly meet. The city lies below me, the strange, half-modern, half-ancient, fanatical old burg which has wrapped about it the great

folds of a Moslem sack-cloth in penance
for sins imaginary, yet no less real.
The illusions of the mind before such
scenes are firm and convincing. It is so
easy to be resigned, religious, believing
under such tranquil, peace-giving inspiration.

IX.

The Negro. The Negro type, which
is to be met with here in
its several phases of evolution and inter-
transfusion with the ruling element of
the country, is one which will bear close
scrutiny, and be found not wanting in
interest. To us free-born and free-con-
ditioned Americans, the negro is ever
an object of regard, and often of our
veneration, since he, for whose prosperity
we have suffered and for whose welfare
we have paid so dearly, naturally grows
precious in our eyes. Even here, where
slavery has denied the negro the com-
monest opportunities of education, there
is to be found, not unoften, types of certain nobility—genuine spirits whose
black masks have not concealed any of
the benignity so inherent, and toward

whom it is but our manly duty to ex-
tend a hearty regard. Never before
have "God's images cut in ebony" as-
sured me of the dignity of their race as
here in subjugation, where the very feeling that they are in no wise equals
gives additional quality to their best
efforts. We expect much of princes and
rich men's sons. We expect little of
slaves. The former can never outride
our anticipations; the latter may often
put us to blush that for a nonce we mis-
conceived the inherent equality. As for
the negress, she is something of a superior creature, even though she be not
fattened by the stuffing process that
her unfortunate mistress endures. She
is statuesque in figure, graceful oftentimes in the arrangement of her pink costume, and particularly pert while reclin-
ing at ease, with something of the tigress
in the lassitude of her repose. The silver rings upon her dusky ankles and
arms are far more ornamental than they
would be upon white skin, and the pretty
kerchiefs of silk surrounding the head
like an aureole of light, gives something
distinguished to the whole outline—

something even supernatural at times. Another marked distinction between the negress and her Arab mistress, is the gaiety which is permitted her, and which here is sorely unbecoming in a woman of whiter complexion. They are always cheerful and happy, seemingly, and doubtless their black faces are the only light of the household, since the painful reserve and absolute withdrawal of their mistresses from the outer world makes the depths of *ennui* and disgust with uneventful life nearly maddening.

X.

The Bazaars again. The indescribable scenes in and about the Arab bazaars, fill one with the true spirit of the fallen ages. The narrow streets are thatched, save here and there, at some important Five Points, or celebrated Arab Seven Dials, where one catches a happy glimpse of the blue sky; and although it is noisy in the extreme, it is the noise of human voices— the din and concatenation of buyers and sellers in long shiny bournouses, with lean shoulders, and airs of abstraction

alternating the feline scrutiny of passing affairs when trickery is suspected.
In this uncertain twilight even at noonday, the wide labyrinth of streets and
lanes beginning everywhere, ending nowhere, are filled to overflowing with the
faithful and the infidel; the former all
the way from Damascus to London, the
latter from St. Petersburg to San Fran-
cisco. We meet many Europeans in
Arab dress, a fact which enables us to
understand how thorough a knowledge
of this Eastern life many of the literary,
and particularly the artistic, lights of
the cultured world have been privileged. The little shops or stalls along
the sides of these long passages look
more like niches in the walls of some
cathedral, where sits in abject apathy
a bournoused saint, surrounded, as it
were, by offerings. But once manifest
an interest in the little trinkets about the
shopkeeper—the inlaid Arab firearms
of ancient shape and perhaps workmanship ; the silk-veil merchant, or sandal
dealers, the moment a prospective purchaser approaches, and particularly a
giaour, the Arab, who would spit into his

face upon the slightest provocation, and
denominate him "Christian dog," now
is attentive to his wants. These little
booths are in groups; the leather booths
where all sorts of quaint Arab capari-
sons, shining and barbaric, flash out to
greet the beholder, are by themselves,
as are the niches where silks for the
draperies of the wives and favorites are
sold, and the stores of every other conceivable variety. Only the little apothecary and toy shops seem to ignore their
brethren in the trade ; here the quaint
little niches, where on the walls are long
rows of bottles, boxes and jars, and
everything from *henna* to leeches may be
had, to the latter, where the little ones
lead their indulgent mammas, and are
regaled with nick-nacks of a quality and
crudeness of workmanship and design
that would be ignored by any of our
modern sons and daughters of indulgent
America.

Now and then the approach to a brass-
worker's shop is heralded by a ceaseless
din, and a most picturesque glimpse of
the workingmen at their arts is afforded
us. These little shops, where quaint

Arabesques are pounded out with such charming delicacy upon plates and pots for table and toilet use, remind one of the little brass-worker's shops of Venice, near the Santa Marguerita. Aside from the noisy spots, the bazaars are comparatively quiet places of trade, and one almost misses the sound of horses' hoofs, the crack of whips and the rumble of wagons—the familiar hubbub of modern business life in our lands. Then other unfamiliar sights greet the traveler every now and then. The religious fanatic, heralded by drums and tambourines, and followed by a motley mob of Moslem worshippers ; the beggars, covered with filth, and lepers holding out their shrunken, ashen, pallid limbs eaten to the bone with disease, voices husky and sepulchral, and visages ghastly in abject abandon to the ravages of the disease. Then, perhaps, not the least interesting to foreigners, the sorcerers and magicians performing their incantations and mysterious feats of black art astonishing to the novice and seemingly no less to the vulgar crowd which gathers about, enjoying perhaps for the hundredth time, at another's expense, the quick machinations of the priest-like magician and the daring of the snake-charmer. And now and then,  as if to vary still more the brilliant picture, through some door ajar, one catches a glimpse of a group of festive dancing girls in the seclusion of the marble court, where, in the center of a circle of maidens, each manipulating a tom-tom, a sort of mandolin or other instrument, accompanied by a weird minor falsetto, a pretty figure draped in flowing garments in happy contrast with her sisters, dances gracefully and lithely with feather-like step and wave-like motion, seemingly enraptured with her own presence of loveliness.

How astonishingly like a dream is all
this southern wonderland ! How far es-
stranged from such a life, such a sphere,
such a political and social state as ours !
The imperturbable, ceaseless pulse of this
great people is as little in unison with
the quick beat of our modern system as
is the sluggish creep of the armadillo
like the leap of the stag. Starvation, qui-
escence—death : activity, progress, life !
They understand us so little, or rather
misunderstand us so much, that they do
not even comprehend the reason of our
caring to study their ways and manners.
Foreigners are objects of their passing curiosity, perhaps, of their cupidity
always, but of their serious interest
never. The great brown *capouchon*, and
the white, faultless veil, both draw
down into most dreamy solitude the
despiser of everything new, the hater
of everything foreign. Not even the
shrill, fierce cry of " Bâleuk—bâleuk ! "
which causes them to stand aside for a
dignitary and his attendants to pass by,
give them anything more than a passing
concern, and on they plod in their day-
dreams, unconscious, apathetic, as in a

trance of ecstasy. Then, in the midst
of all this mercantile activity, obeying
the command of the muezzin, business is
for the moment suspended and the shrill
funereal tones of the priest on the minaret proclaim the hour and lament the
vanity of all earthly things. This cry,
heard in the small hours of the night, is
mystifying indeed, where four-fifths of
the faithful are asleep, and probably but
one-fifth of the remaining one-fifth, give
it more than a passing heed ; but here
in the busy heart of the day to hear the
wild, solemn chant rising and falling
upon the gentle southern wind, now as
if delivering a curse, now as if summon-
ing up the whole nation's strength into
one unbounded psalm of praise, is mystifying in the extreme. So conservative,
so loving toward their offspring, so hating
and intolerant of Christians and despis-
ing of the Jew, so inexplicable in the
mazes of goodness and vituperation, with
all their religious fervor and sincerity to
sharpen the strange southern portrait
and give intensity to all they say and
do, surely the Arabs are living paradoxes
to the most scrutinizing foreign eyes.

XI.

New Scenes Again. We left Algiers by rail early Tuesday morning, after having been regaled with coffee and rolls, the milk for the former being supplied by the goats that are driven from door to door, picturesque Algerian women and boys the custodians. The railroad bears around the beautiful blue bay in a north-easterly direction, the splendid villas dotting the hillsides here and there looking like opals in the rose tints of the early morning, contrasting with the rich background of verdure which half encloses them. The French have done much to improve Algeria, but it is an evident fact that they are no colonizers as compared with the English. They stopped effectually the civil wars of the petty chiefs of the Arabs — the ignoble skirmishing which cost the able ranks a severe diminution the country could ill afford. They have also built a very good railroad from Oran to Tunis—the whole length of Algeria—some other roads from the sea inland, and otherwise developed the

country. They have established small
viliages as refuges to receive the loyal
families of Alsace and Lorraine, after
the forced possession taken of that disputed district by the Germans ; but as a
general thing these magnanimous and
patriotic asylums have not been a success. Only one of these villages seems
to be in flourishing activity, leaving
the remainder to effectually illustrate
the folly of attempting to cork a bottle
with a stone ; or in other words, of sup-
plying a *desideratum* in a tropical province with the cold, solid, unsupple character of the mountainous, middle Europe.

Through tunnels and down the length
of deep cañons and gorges we sped,
the scene on each hand one of con-
tinued picturesque beauty. Now we pass
a bright foaming cascade, the waters
leaping down the ragged edge of the
mountain with a cool, joyous sound ;
now we glide by a Kabyle village, or
contemplate from a distance a flock of
sheep and goats in the valley, watched

by their half-savage shepherd. The
Kabyle villages on the top of the mountain ridges, with their brush wigwams
and brush fences to keep off the wild
animals, look as African and uncivilized
as anything we have yet seen. Terrible
tragedies are related with regard to the
destruction and the murder of the
French colonists by the Arabs and the
fiercer natives of the Kabyle tribe in
their last revolt of 1871.

XII.

The Journey. At a village, which had
but a passing charm for
us—so passing that the altitudinous condition of the thermometer did not
warrant our venturing from under
cover—we were given a very good
breakfast. The country about has been
even in recent times infested with lions,
and certainly a starving brood of beasts
they must be that remain, for passing
up through the mountains the country
is like the back of a hedgehog—a sort of
greyish dull neutral tint which belies the
fact that ever grain or vegetable made

effort to glorify its Maker there. Still,
there are patches of oats and barley, and
now and then we see a brace of Arabs in
the blazing sun, girdled with a rag
about the waist, the rest of the body
bronzed and bare, swinging the sickle
with an ease that is as graceful a motion
as the stroke of the oar of the Venetian
gondolier. The thermometer stands
125° or thereabouts, and gives one a
rare opportunity of testing the Northern
blood, and of purifying it by boiling.
The West is to be congratulated. I
do not wonder that the oriental wor-
ships fire, and that Mahommet performed so many miracles by its aid.
I think I should turn Thalian if I lived
here through the hot months, recognizing
heat as the source of creation. Now
and then we pass a Roman ruin to remind us of the Cæsars whose triumphs
have left records from Brittany to Persia—records which here, he must be
a sturdy antiquarian, indeed, who invades for new classic light. The little
towns are very similar, the trim French
soldiers and the slovenly, but highly
picturesque Arab, making confusion in

the observance of old types. At Selif we pass a great market where the Kabyles from the mountains, the Arabs from the plains, and even the nomadic Saharans from the desert oases, meet to exchange their various products, making a scene of indescribable effect of light and shadow, color and detail.

We were glad to reach Constantine at midnight, after a journey over the hot plains and mountain plateaus since five o'clock in the morning. There was nothing of very serious discomfort to mar the flight into Tunis, having the whole compartment in the car to ourselves to lounge about at our serene complacency. We found Constantine a characteristic city of the western Orient, perched upon a high rocky plateau, surrounded by deep, dark ravines resembling the huge cañons of the Colorado. It is a natural fortress, and in times previous to Krupp guns that hurl a projectile for miles, must have been a keep almost impregnable. The former name was Cirta ; but A.D. 313 the present appellation, Constantine, was adopted, and for a number of years thereafter it main-

tained itself as a sort of independent republic.   About the old Roman ruins are
many   noteworthy   relics   of   interest.
The walls and crevices of the tumble-
down relics are the homes of innumerable birds with a shrill pipe, and here
and there at the ancient cistern patched
up for modern use, the Arab women
and girls tread clothes with their feet,
to   perform   the   homely   ablutionary
duty which in our land is done by machine.   An old Roman mill of infinite
picturesqueness,   also   patched   up   for
modern use, is in full operation.   The
Arab quarter is as usually suggestive,
the native as persistent in his gentle-
manly habits of laziness as elsewhere,
heroically giving over to the women the
drudgery which would otherwise conflict
with his daily long and deliberate cog-
itations upon man and nature, which
philosophical rhapsodies, judging from
the gravity of each sheik's demeanor,
means the salvation of the whole race.
Constantine is a place noted for the lon-
gevity of its inhabitants, but it is a sad
fact that though there are fifteen tomb-
stones here recording the ages of de-

ceased from 100 to 132 years, the whole world does not flock hither, convincing us that the poor mortal would not live always.

The *muezzin* in his minaret not far from our rooms aroused us from our slumbers by his dreamy call of *"Allah, iesa merua, Allah!"* calling the faithful to worship. I arose and went to the window. The city was wrapped in slumber, and the lone figure on the tower, with his hands extended and his upturned face against the pale moonlight, made a weird and enchanting effect. Then we heard his shuffling sandals clatter, clatter down the stone steps—a curiously contrasting sound, almost humorous in the way he is supposed to frighten off the devils with a premonition of his approach—and soon we heard his voice again repeating the solemn injunction from the top of another tower in a distant part of the city.

Our route was to lead us to Biskera, the oasis on the desert approached from this point, but meeting a sirocco blowing fiercely from the burning sands, we were glad to abandon the project. A sight of the great rolling waste of sand-

sky was so heartily crushing to our usually good spirits, that we concluded to
leave this part of our interesting journey
to the chronicles of the past, which have
never been so glowing that they have en-
ticed the traveller into the desert for
mere novelty.

XIII.

Carthage. The country between
Constantine and the city
of Tunis is much like Algiers—dry
plains, plateaus, brush huts and moving
caravans against the milk-white sky of
the afternoon. On leaving Tunis some
hours later, the moonlight shining
through the great arches of the ancient
aqueduct delights us with an effect
most weird and estranging. What a
stupendous piece of engineering the
aqueduct must have been. Think of
bearing water from the mountains of
Zaghoan, a distance of sixty miles, over
a great stone water course that conveyed
seven millions of gallons per day into
the great walled city of Carthage.
How rich did this one fountain of God

makes this beautiful city, its gardens and suburbs ! Surely it is an inspiring thought that is prompted at sight of these great stone arches which stand out in the pale moonlight like "the branched vertebræ of some gigantic serpent," to adopt the pointed simile of Sir Greenville Temple. The great Hadrian, under whose instruction so many huge and splendid feats of architecture and science took form, certainly outdid himself in this superb feat of engineering. The great wall of Britain, from the Solway Firth to the Tyne, the great Temple to the Olympian Venus which Pisistratus had left unfinished seven hundred years before, the lovely gardens and villa at Tivoli, the great Roman masses of masonry known as Hadrian's pile, and other majestic relics, leave traces of his gigantic intellect, cold and politic as it was in every degree.

Tunis

VIII.

" A thousand raps on the door ; but alas ! few invitations
to ' walk in.' "—*A Moorish Saying.*

" I brought you good-will and a blessing ; I carry back
a blessing and good-will."—*From the Arabic.*

" Salâm aleyk !" — Peace be with you ! — *Bedouin
Salute.*

TUNIS.

The city of Tunis is composed of Jews and Mahommedans in about equal numbers, French and Maltese also in about equal numbers, and a scattering population of Greeks, Italians and Germans. It stands on an isthmus, separating two saline bodies of water; the salt bed of the drained pit is like a desert of blazing white sand. The Bar-el-Bey, or palace

of the Bey of Tunis—that splendidly
housed prisoner of war—we were dis-
appointed to find a gross, uninteresting strcture, quite out of happy proportions, externally.   The interior, however, with the exception of the modern
French part which is in ugly imitation
of the ugly meretricious art of Louis
the Sixteenth, is profuse in Moorish decorations, which in parts seem to have
rivalled even the great Spanish Alhambra.
There is a lamentable lack of taste and
the sense for congruities when compar-
ing the modern qualities of decoration
with the ancient and more noble.   We
were interested in the paintings on the
walls, portraits of Louis XVI., Napolean
III., and the Bey of Tunis ; but especially interesting to us, as may be imagined, was the fine, full-length portrait
of George Washington, whose kind face
looked down from the canvas as benignantly and noble as ever, compelling us
to take off our hats in reverence.   The
Moorish decorations of the ceiling, the
marble sculpture of figures and various
devises of antiquity, were extremely interesting.

The new palace, not far distant, does not inspire one with much regard, save as an ethical revelation illustrating forcibly the ignominy of political downfall. This, as well as the former palace, was built for the Beys of Tunis ; but both are now kept up in a certain respectability, their tawdry chambers desolate and musty with neglect and decay, their harems and baths untenanted and left in charge of lazy servants—everything that bespeaks the completeness of the invader's subjugation of the conquered. The present Bey has lived during the nine years of French protectorship, at Marsa, and is really a prisoner of state, like a Maha Rajah of India, the real king being the French commandant or Resident General. The Bey for his superb figure-headship, as one might say, receives the munificent salary of one hundred thousand francs per month—something like a quarter of a million dollars per annum. This is a sort of bribe to keep him and his Arab adherents, who fret and chafe under the galling yoke of subjection, within peace-bounds. Other chiefs, it is said, receive large salaries as blood-money to keep them from mutual and general mutiny.

The Bey's palace at Marsa we did not visit. This place of magnificent captivity stands on a fine eminence commanding a delicious view of the sober, blue Mediterranean. There, with his three hundred wives and concubines, and his body-guards to keep up the appearance of power, the royal potentate takes life serenely, enjoying all the honor of a king with none of his responsibilities.

XV.

Fattening the Women. We have seen here and in the city of Tunis, many of the handsome Jewish belles, dressed in their peculiar style, which would be very pretty were their forms not so short and stocky, their lower limbs measuring almost the circumference of the waist. Corpulency is the distinction desirable to be attained by Tunisian women to gratify the masculine taste, and they are raised for the matrimonial market with the care that a fatted bullock is for exportation. Their dress is peculiar—at first rather repulsive than otherwise—skin-tight trousers, made of white muslin or silk, short jackets, loose and flowing, and made of some bright snapping color. They are very handsome, particularly the young maidens, with large, quite almond-shaped black eyes, sable-black hair, sallow complexions, and heavy dark eye-brows and fine long lashes. As they parade up and down the Esplanade or lounge about the gardens in front of their homes on the sea-shore, they present a most attractive appearance—more so than any other feminine character we have seen, with the possible exception of the Madileños in the more beautifying mantilla.

In Tunis all the natives seem to be men; and as the Moorish women cannot appear on the street with uncovered faces, a black veil is here used instead of the white of other countries of the southern Mediterranean coast. The Jewish women, on the contrary, seldom go out, except at sunset and after to promenade on the Esplanade, and then they appear as gaudy as a bevy of ballet girls.

The little Jewish children of the upper social ranks are the most artificial caricatures, with their painted eyes, and profusion of gew-gaws of varied brilliancy that heighten the grotesqueness of the portrait ; but the little ones of the middle and lower caste are the most natural and healthful little sunbeams in the world, so unlike their waxy, dollish, upper-caste sisters. One meets them everywhere, yet never wearies of the ever varied tokens of careless *naïveté*, yet intelligence withal, and the light freshness of their roguish countenances amid so much that is gloomy and depressing in these bewildering highways.

I.

To Carthage. We drove out about eight miles northeast to inspect the remains of the ancient, renowned city of Carthage.

> " The rising city which from far you see,
> Is Carthage. . . . "

wrote Virgil when he set forth in flowing numbers the now quite uncertain fact that the Phœnician Dido fled from Tyre to escape her brother's hatred, after that

fierce king had killed Sichæus, Dido's
husband, through jealousy ; but most
insignificant comparatively, are the ruins
of this proud city on approaching by
land or viewing from the sea. The Par-
thenon, so conspicuous from the harbor
of Piræus, the temples and arches so inviting of interest in Rome, the great monasteries of Ai in Balbec and in Thebes,
inspire the approaching traveller with a
sense of awe, and prepare him for a
much higher degree of reverence to follow ; but Carthage, with all its noble
history, is a most ignoble ruin. Fleeing
from Tyre, and landing at the spot later
named Carthage, Dido asked for so
much land as might be enclosed with an
ox-hide. This granted, she proceeded
to cut the hide into threads and enclosed the whole hill-site upon which the
citadel was forthwith built. So goes
the tale, which lacks our personal confir-
mation by the aid of the miserable Bedouins who hibernate or rather infest,
the surrounding lands. But rather certain is it, that though Dido may not
have been the founder of the city, she
was the enlarger and beautifier of it.

The old aqueduct which looked so weirdly imposing as we approached the city of Tunis by moonlight from Constantine, now appeared dry and stupid, in the glare of noonday ; and this and the other ruins are occupied by gypsies by a happy skill of adaptation which only the barbarian, who does not believe in putting too much labor into anything, could improvise. One of the most interesting things was the old Roman mill, which was in operation, a lean old horse drawing the crank-pole, and the stone pestal grinding the meal. The old baths, large enough to bury a regiment or float a couple of gunboats—very like the reservoirs of Solomon near Hebron in the Holy Land, were also indicative of the decay of the times, for, indeed, the present inhabitants of this almost sacred soil, seldom wash; and, moreover, deem it a sin for which they would never be forgiven, to wash an infant before its first birthday. Doubtless this accounts for the terrible statistics of infant mortality among the Bedouins and lower Arabs and Moors, who are fast becoming an extinct race of people.

The old amphitheater and Basilica
are the most imposing of relics here.
The Roman wish has been fulfilled—
Carthage is the most ignominious of
ruins. Everywhere huge blocks of stone
and carved fragments lie about, pillars,
tiles, and sculptures. The location of
Carthage must have been grandeur itself. The sea before it leaping up to the
edge of Dido's palace, the great salt inland lake—back of the eminence the
clear, tropic sky and the Zaghonan
mountains, whence was conveyed the
water to the ancient city, in the distance.
The setting sun cast a vivid glow upon
the vast heap of a once noble metropolis, and later, the moon came up over
the mountain across the bay, sweeping
a wide golden path along the calm waters, the air was cool and refreshing after
the dull lassitude of the hot day, and
thus delighted with the happy finale of
our historical drama, we drove back to
the city.

As we approached Tunis, we met the
carriage of the Bey, closely covered, and
were told that it contained some important personage of the Bey's harem.

A Celebration. Early Sunday morning, the Bey was to arrive amidst the military splendor and the firing of cannon, to attend the reception given in honor of the French celebration of the foundation of the republic, July 14. Like our Independence Day, it is a day of great festivity and rejoicing. Flags, bunting, and in the evening, illuminations and fireworks, made merry all hearts, save those of the dethroned Moors and Arabs. They cheered lustily for their Bey, as he came into the city in a carriage drawn by six horses, where he reviewed the six thousand soldiers at this point—cavalry, zouaves and various companies. The Moors, in their long flowing robes and distinguished head-gear, looked picturesque enough to be really worthy of their own rule. When their grand outcast king had gone by, they looked sullen and grave, and soon retired into their strange seclusion, to brood, doubtless, upon the present unhappy condition of things for the invaded, and the fortune of the invaders.

The Bey is very politic, however, and uses his strong and subtle influence to keep the subjugated in a state of peace, knowing the futility of resistance.

II.

The Child of the Past.   It is a convincing fact that the Arab's social regime is impregnable to the innovations of modern life and convenience. Capable of perceiving the delicate shades of the ideal, with a climate that renders most acutely resonant every intellectual fibre, and with a language whose expanse and richness bear all the refinements and indications of a high order of social life, the Arab is one and apart from the rest of mankind. He is too deeply rooted in the arbitrary convictions begotten of his forefathers, to believe in aught that combats them. While all the world has progressed, worshipped the present and looked out for the future, the Arab has glorified the past like a true apostle of his creed, gainsaid nothing that his social scripture had denominated true, and while he has turned his back on the present, his enemies have circumscribed him completely. Modern wealth, manners, refinements and the meanest comforts of conventional life have engendered no new quality which is recognizable in his contemporary art or science. He is one calm, unbending, unassimilating repetend of old fact foibles; and any one who invades this relic of his forefathers, is the meanest of triflers. His skill lies not in the resolving his social life into pictorial light, but rather in the hidden and mystical significance of things. Unconsciously, no doubt, the Arab is the subtilest Platonist, physically fragile, morally an extremest, mentally brilliant but implacable, and altogether most affectionate and ferocious. He has nothing of the synthethical, but bears all the faults and a few of the virtues of the analytical faculty. He sees no connections between his own sensitive nature and the external condition that is the result of his short-sighted analysis. Hence is it that the Northern reasoner—the cold, calculating analyzer with his disciplined acquisitiveness and his ductile morals,

has touched the dreamer to waking;
but only to wake him into a knowledge
of his own slavery.

The Arab is a splendid study now
only as a superb barbarian whose chiefest virtue is his splendid conservatism.
The barbarian, like the highest type of
the physical and intellectual man, is an
intensely absorbing study ; the mediocre
man only is utterly a point of abandon-
ment. The barbarian is usually a type
—a concise abridgment of old customs
and obsolescent usage through which
the observer may look into the dim but
certain outlines of a thousand years before him ; the highly civilized man, on
the contrary, is the product of a race
which, in its steady ascendency has cast
aside superstions for the arts ; the ideal
for the actual ; synthesis for analysis ;
the abstract for the severely concrete; and
the ideal, in a measure, for the material,
yet with all the virtues of the former retained. He, too, is assuredly interesting
—more so by far than the barbarian ;
but the middle man—that uncertain,
vacillating product of a society waking
from the dregs of despotism into the

light of republicanism, from the depth
of intellectual torpor of restriction into
the freedom of voice which is far more
exultant than artistic, boisterous than
refined—this mediocre man just crossing
the intermediate strip of land between
the natural barbarian and his splendid
contemporary, is most despairingly void
of interest.   He has not the innate nobility of the highest type, and lacks even
the virtue of being an interesting barbarian.   What the conventional man
sees is the great broad surface of life.
Nothing above, nothing below this plane
gives him more than a passing concern.
Put an Arab in trousers, and what a
sorry dog have you made of what was
once characteristic and bold.   Likewise
clothe your higher type of man in
a grey bournouse, or a deer-skin after
the manner of your Sioux Indian, and
what a grotesque anomaly have you
made of this once dignified and noble
condition.

This much is said primarily to prove
that the French occupation of Tunis will
never make the Arab a Frenchman, nor
the Frenchman an Arab.   The second

thought is the lamentably evident one :
that the Arab, like the North American
Indian, with all his delightful character,
his mystery, his nobility and his dignified setting of an old and precious picture, must go. The world is too large
for him. Once his kingdom was a continent ; then the waters crept up till the
broad area became an island. Soon it
becomes a pinnacle—then it disappears.
The anomalous individual will be
merged into the conventional mass : the
spring shall continue to bubble, but only
at the bottom of a great sea.

III.

Adieu to Tunis.   We left Tunis in a blaze
of splendor on the night
of the 14th of July, when fireworks, illuminations, firing of cannon and the festivities, strongly in character with those of
our 4th of July, were in order. One of
the notable events of the day was the
fantasia of the Arabs on the plaza—a
most dazzling series of barbarian feats
upon the horse by a company of be-
spangled Moors, mounted lustily upon

richly caparisoned steeds which were trained with admirable discipline. The *fantasia* was accompanied by the unparalleled hubbub of the Arab tambourines, clapping of hands and shrill pipes, together with an unabated amount of enthusiasm on the part of all the spectators. We took the train to La Goulette, the port of Tunis, about eight miles distant from the latter city, which dependant borough is built almost entirely of the wreckage of ancient Carthage. Tunis itself does not escape the charge of vandalism, be it known, and not unoften do we come upon dignified and noble sentiments carved upon stone which once consecrated the entrances of Carthagenian temples, and which now beam forth from the lintels of miserly looking Arab hovels in the heart of the city.

The sail to Malta was one of unparalleled beauty, the variable color of the calm waters defying the skill of art with their variegated hues and gentle inweavings of color and contrast. It seems so strange to be at last beyond the sights and sounds of Moorish character—the

shrill "Bâleuk !" of the slave of the dignitary making room through the crowded street for his mounted master, the
supreme dignitary ; the bray of mules
and the hoarse brawl of the camels ; the
shrill, mournful piping of the Arab folk-
song and the accompaniment thereto
with voices of weirdest, clear-ringing
cadence in unchangeable minors ; and
last of all, that funereal, all commanding
cry like a voice from eternity—the call
to prayers of the *muezzin* on the minaret
who speaks words in spirit intelligible
even to us who do not understand the
letter, words like the knell over the
grave of all that is good and worthy,
leaving us all the more bound to live and
act full complete lives in the present
when the great uncertainty of the future
lies upon our right and our left hand.

To the west a pretty island lifts from
the waters as by magic—a lustrous
" pearl set in a silver sea," the towers on
its summits casting strange elongated
shadows down to the edge of the waters,
and the wheeling gulls venturing ever
nearer the wreckage of some fish boats
beyond. The sharp profile against the

twilight gives it a spectral appearance, and robs it of its homely commonplace. A banker of Tunis—a very pleasing gentleman—gave us much valuable information regarding the natives of the country he was so proud to own as the land of his birth. He confided to us the story of his winning the love of a young American lady from Delaware, who was travelling with her parents in Africa some years ago, and who afterwards became his wife. Although his sons had received their education in America, neither his wife nor himself had been there since their marriage. " We are anticipating with much pleasure a visit to your country," said he, " and shall probably live for a time in southern California, having heard such glowing accounts of its climate." " How strange it appears," I replied, " that our people come to Algiers and Tunis to enjoy the benefits of your wonderful climate, while your people express a desire to visit our country for a like reason. It is the old story over again. Something better in some other place than our own."

Our conversation drifted toward the

subject of the Arabs and his experience
with them.   " People only glancing at
the race with the superficial observation
of a tourist," said he, " mistake the
Arabs to be a wild and warlike people ;
when in reality they are remarkably
tractable, and in social life gentle and
kind.   They are boastful and assuming
to a degree oftentimes, but true to the
oriental spirit, strangely exaggerating
in everything.   He called to mind an incident that had occurred directly under
his observation : " An Arab was commanded by a former Bey, for some meri-
torious service to his sovereign, to fill
some important position under the government. The fortunate courtier changed
his wild *fellahin* dress for the robes of
royalty as befitting his state, and I was
present when he first appeared in the
rôle of minister before his sovereign.
He made an eloquent speech upon re-
ceiving his appointment, and from that
time became a trusted and popular *aide*
to the monarch, amassing something of
a fortune as well.   Then came death and
a change of rulers, and the Arab was deposed, his whole fortune being confis-

cated. It was then that the nobility of the man as superior to his position was manifest ; for he went back to his plow, assuming the native dress and manner with characteristic courage, and took up his simple mode of life again without a murmur."

He said that the Arabs, as a rule, have a wonderful faculty of catching hold of an eloquent turn of thought or happy phrase, but true to this theory of brilliance, are superficial in attainments, full of superstition, necromancy and sorcery. He calls upon the present Bey of Tunis, but his impression of the ruler is that he is childish and has too much faith in his court sorcerers. "Nothing serious or worthy can come of Arab diplomacy and social life till their girls are differently educated," he was pleased to say. "The training of the children is entrusted to incompetent females who fill their young minds with senseless romance and superstition, and nothing womanly and heroic can come of such pollution and ignorance."

He said that his wife often visits the harems of the Bey, and is kindly received. I asked him about the rule requiring the native women to cover their faces in the street and elsewhere, not allowing any but their lords to look upon them. He said that their social law was very strict in this respect, "and why not ?" he added with characteristic emphasis, "it is most necessary; for Arab women, you must know, are not women, but females ! "

An instance of the stubborn stupidity with which this law is enforced, came under his observation. A very beautiful and accomplished young lady, the daughter of a dignitary, was very ill and a French physician of Tunis was called in, as a last resort, to prescribe for her. The bed was shielded by a screen, through which the patient's hand was thrust. The physician felt her pulse and said : " This young woman has a high, dangerous fever of some kind, and I must see her face, or I can do nothing for her. There was a long and serious consultation on the part of the father and the members of the household, after which the father returned to the physician and replied ; "No ; I would rather my daughter should die than that you should look upon her face ! " and in a very short time she passed away.

Injustice of French Taxation. The Arabs are under an unusual oppression of taxes under the French, and to me it seems a great mistake pecuniarily on the part of the governors, to say nothing of the injustice to the Arabs. North Africa is an agricultural country and nothing else. The olive trees were formerly productive, and their cultivation was a great industry till the French placed a local tax of sixty per cent on all the oil produced here, and as a result, the farmers cut down their olive orchards, as they cannot produce it with such a high tax. Tobacco culture might be another occupation, were it not for the fact that the home tax is so great that it is far cheaper to import from America.

And so we take our journey home-
ward from the lands of the Bey and Sultan, thankful at heart for all the kind-
ness received at the hands of many, who,
other than the common good will man
to man, had no object in view save to
give us happiness. It is gratifying indeed to receive on every hand such
marks of respect as has been often our
good fortune, in places where we had no
reason to expect more than a common
business courtesy. It proves to us that
an American, with his frank ways, generous opinions in toleration of all that is
honestly and devoutly believed in, may
travel the wide world over and inspire
respect in the hearts of those whose language, customs, traditions and religions,
are entirely distinct from, and even at
variance, with his own.

Appendix.

APPENDIX.

NOTE I.—The Antiquity of Bull-Fighting.

Although personally I heartily condemn, and find very
few reasons to extenuate indulgence in, the wretched sport
of bull-fighting in Spain, there are several interesting data
which offer themselves to the student of Spanish history
and antiquity, and that of other countries where the sport
has been countenanced, and a few of these facts I have
taken the liberty to append here. To an American the
spectacle is thoroughly disgusting; but likewise to the
student of men, the antiquity of the brutal sport is of
healthful and natural interest.

The antiquity of Tauromachian art appears to be a matter of much conjecture. It has been creditably argued
that it is of Thessalian origin, and that Julius Cæsar imported the sport from Greece for the edification of his subjects; that the Moors assumed the science from the Romans, bringing it to the high degree of spectacular effect
which has been emulated by their more agile and skilful

followers. Passages in Libey and Festus would lead us to infer that the *Ludi Tauralia* were games instituted in honor of certain anniversary events, as were the Olympian games in Sparta; but from Servius and Varro we learn that these were religious observances, and certain gymnastic exercises performed by men wrapped in the pelts of bulls. We also learn that Tarquinius Superbus instituted a form of religious penance which might lead us to believe that the Taurobolia were merely bull-pits. Silius makes note of the games of Scipio into which the Andalusians took part; and Suetonius gives a detailed account of a series of gladiatorial and other festivities beginning with the Eastern, probably Median, games, and ending with those of Andalusia, which doubtless were the matching of bulls against bulls, rather than against men. Iberian coins bear the images of bulls, which might have been the emblem of Osiris, in Spain worshipped as Hercules, or of Astarte, rather than emblems of Tauromachian triumph. Humboldt made a journey to Biscay to study the Oscan inscriptions, and the sculptured alto-relievo discovered in the ruins of Clunia, which represented various scenes, leading one to believe bull-fighting to be of Iberian origin. However, of the Thessalian origin of the dangerous sport there is ample evidence. Philippus, the Thessalian poet, describes the exact manner of parrying and overwhelming the ferocious bulls in the ring, in exact accordance with the rules laid down to the modern *Picadores*. A *denarius*, a small coin of Thessaly, bears the image of a fierce bull with the impression of the head of Cæsar on the converse. Claudius, and his successor, Nero, instituted games similar to bull-fighting, records of which are extent. Wilkinson, in his learned work on the manners and customs of ancient 'gypt, proves clearly that combats of men against men c:

foot, and against bulls, were known in the remotest period
to the Pharoahs, and substantiates a theory from sculptures
on certain tombs at Beni Hassan and Thebes. Bull-pens,
and other appurtenances of the amphitheatres at Murviedro,
at Murida and Italica, prove that bull-fights were common
there. At Avila, on a certain marriage festival in 1107, a
bull-fight was celebrated, in which Moors and Christians
both fought ; and in 1124, at Saldana, when Alphonso VII.,
of the Count of Barcelona, a similar festivity took place,
according to Moratin, in his *Origen de las fiestas de toros.*
The conquest of Andalusia, in the thirteenth century, set-
tled Granada as a point of headquarters for bull-fighters.
We learn from Alphonso the Wise, that the clergy were
prohibited from viewing, and Christians were prohibited
from takir.g part, in the combats, which lead us to believe
that only Moors participated. Gibbon gives an account of
a combat celebrated in the year 1332, in the colliseum at
Rome, "after the fashion of the Moors," so that the Romans appear to have borrowed from Spain the very sport
which it is well contended was imported from Rome into
Andalusia. And so down from the thirteenth century, we
find records of bull-running and bull-fighting, with
methods more or less barbarous and unskilful, till 1440,
where we find in Baston's letters that " there is one coming
to England, a knight out of Spain, the which knight will
run a course with a sharp spear, etc.," which may account
for the bull-bating custom of England, mentioned by Fitz
Stephen and Hentzner, who declared that bull and bear-
baiting were popular sports with the London youth in the
time of William the Third. A curious phrase is to be found
in the letters to Lord Colchester, in which Howell gives an
account of this " chiefest of all Spanish sports. Commonly
there are men killed at it ; therefore there are priests ap-

pointed to be there to confess to them. It hath happened
oftentimes, that a bull hath taken up two men upon his
horns, with their entrails dangling about them. As I am
told, the Pope hath sent divers bulls against this sport of
bulling, yet it will not be felt, the nation hath taken such an
habitual delight in it."

In the life of the reverend Father Bennet, of Canfilde,
1623, is the following sarcastic observation that: "Even
Sunday is a day designed for beare-bayting, and even the
howre of theyre (the Protestants) service is allotted to it;
and indeed, the tyme is as well spent at the one as at the
other," which does not argue well for the enthusiasm of
the church in the time of James the First. Good Queen
Elizabeth certainly enjoyed the bear-baiting entertainment
at Killingsworth, in 1575, a curious account of which is in
Laneham's account, which begins: " Well, Syr, the Bearz
wear brought foorth intoo the Court, etc.," which, when
the battle was well begun, continues with vigor, "therefore, with fending and prooving, with plucking and tug-
ging, skratting and byting, by plain tooth and nayll a to
side and toother, such expens of blood and leather waz
thear between them az a moonth's licking, I ween, wyl
not recoover."

NOTE II.—Anecdotes of Velasquez.

There is, however, one unvarying rule with regard to the
real greatness of a master, which makes Murillo in many
respects the superior man. The artist who has no imitators
is but a master of situations already achieved by others.
Few are the imitators of Velasquez, so tremendous an imi-
tator himself, but the followers of the style of Murillo are
legion. A prodigious number of works represented to be

by him, are proven to be those of his pupils and contemporaries. Of Velasquez there is a pretty anecdote in Cum-
berland's Spanish Painters. King Philip had fitted up a
painting room especially to the convenience of his favorite,
to which chamber the king alone, beside the painter, had
access. Velasquez had just finished a portrait of Don
Adrian Pulido, Admiral of the king's fleet. This officer
was under orders to repair to the command of the fleet,
when Philip entered Velasquez's studio, and mistaking
the portrait for the admiral himself, entered into a violent
expostulation for daring to disobey his sovereign's orders.
It was only upon touching the portrait with his hand that
he could be convinced that it was indeed not he whom he
believed it.

Another, perhaps more widely quoted anecdote, sets forth
the woes and final triumph of the slave of Velasquez, who,
noting the fact that the king, on his visits to his famous
courtier, demanded to inspect every canvas which stood on
the floor, face to the wall, conceived the plan of substitut-
ing one of his own ambitious studies, done during his master's *siestas*, for one of those by the painter himself. The
king demanded to see it, and commenting upon its merit,
was astounded upon being told by the slave on bended
knee, that, living so closely in contact with such genius, he
had imbibed of his master's quality, and had performed
this in evidence of it. The king bade him rise and com-
mended him to the artist who was no less astonished and
pleased ; and the slave, now a freedman, was no less a
personage than Paresa, who afterwards became distinctly
eminent in portraits.

Every style of painting then known, sooner or later found
in Velasquez an expositor, and the teacher was even superior to his text. Titian, Greco, and Claude, in landscape,

Salvator and the Dutch contemporaries, all poured into that
gigantic mould their peculiar metals which came forth
with the stamp of his Spanish mintage. From the highest
historical situations to the most commonplace detail of
gypsy low life, his genius was all things to all men. Now
it is a farm-yard, with fowls and cattle, and a deep Andalusian sky ; now the deep blue distances and the mellow,
royal colors of the drapery of his portrait of Philip. How
striking was the antipodal character of these two friends
and contemporaries, Murillo and Velasquez ! The former,
within the four walls of a sacristy of Seville, idealizing
with devotional enthusiasm, painting saints and angels
floating upon ethereality, and attaining the highest degree
of perfection in the art which has the church for its patron ;
and on the other hand, the latter painter on the balcony of
the royal palace of Madrid, portraying in cold, silvery
tones, the last rays of the sun upon the distant range of
Guadarrama, or in the great halls of his king and friend,
eminently the man of tact and diplomacy, brilliant, worldly,
far-seeing and indefatigable.

But whether or not Murillo was the painter of angels,
and Velasquez the painter of men—whether or not the great
estranged, ethereal genius of the former was as a bright iridescent bubble to the substantial, devoted worldiness of
the latter,—it remains a fact that Murillo's works are pre-
eminently expressive ; and " it is for the expressive talents,"
as Henry James says of Daudet, " that we feel an affection."
Murillo answers this demand. Seldom do we find a
man with more than one great idea. Michael Angelo was
one, Donatello was most surely another, Leonardo da
Vinci, the man whom both Draper and Hallam pronounced
to have been " of knowledge almost preternatural," who

anticipated Castelli on the laws of hydraulics, and foreshadowed one of the greatest hypotheses of geology—the elevation of continents, and who carried these great weights of learning with the ease with which he painted " The Last Supper," was without dispute another of the world's rare men of more than one idea. Still, Reubens had but one, and he was great. A magnificent piece of flesh was the heighth and breadth of his theme, and beyond it, either spiritually or with the passion of tragedy or comedy, he could not discern any available material. Velasquez was the intellectual painter with but one idea; Murillo, the rhapsodist with a higher idea, considered poetically, and consequently, a less sure touch and manner, considered technically. While the former could paint the high-born noble, and forget not to reproduce that ineffable distinction which is the result of high-breeding, he took nothing in a higher light than mere realism. He wanted to paint the highest type of the race, and found it in the nobleman. Murillo found his nobles in the street, in the underground hovels—anywhere, taking Nature unawares, and always at her best, her most unguarded moment. Like a clever photographer, who, while pretending to be arranging preliminarily, engages the stiff poser in a genial conversation, and snaps the instantaneous plate at the inspired moment, so Murillo, while we cannot admire him as the giant of technique and perspective that his contemporary was, we love far more, feeling invigorated and perhaps flattered in the presence of his works ; and though we oftentimes do not approve, with true sincerity we applaud, blessing so much appealing sincerity in another.

NOTE III.—Saracenic Philosophy.

It may be pardonable in a discursive narration of personal experiences in Spain, and particularly here in the midst of scenes which seem so redolent of the deep spirit of contemplation familiar to the Mahommedan schoolmen contemporary with the achievements of art and architecture whose remains lie all about us, to touch lightly upon the philosophical development of thought, in contradiction with that which was so zealously religious. In Europe while the scholastic controversy between Nominalism, with Roscellinus as its extreme champion, and Realism, with Anselm as its profound exponent, was warring upon theological dogma which left the polemics at exactly their starting point after forty years of intellectual sparring, the Arabs and the Jewish thinkers, so largely indebted to the Nestorians in Syria, no doubt, were achieving noble things in speculative science in these two cities, Seville and Cordova. Aristotle, already excommunicated by the church of Rome (they did not fear to excommunicate dead philosophers, comets, vermin—anything troublesome whether living or dead, in those times), and the followers of the great Peripatetic threatened with public flagellation, the Saracens amid these hills and by the same rushing waters, were vieing with their Moslem brethren in and about the Calif's court in Bagdad in construing the great Thracian's theories of universals in the interest of the Koran. The first really great thinker who left a profound impression upon his contemporaries and upon scientific thought to the present, was Averroës, who flourished here in Cordova in the twelfth century. He was an Aristotlean with an enthusiasm for his master which amounted to adoration. He took up the theory of evolution with splendid sincerity, arguing logically that creation was merely the "transition from potentiality to actuality." He argued that only the few can obtain high philosophical truth ; that for the rest of mankind, merely a popular creed was the necessity. To him, strangely enough, is the discovery of the spots on the sun attributed. Upon Albertus Magnus, William of Occam, the Franciscan, and even Thomas Acquinas, "the incarnate spirit of scholasticism," the mantle of Averroës fell with an unmistakable aroma of the famous Cordovian clinging to it. This was the *rostra Julia* of all the thinking world. Although the Christians were intolerant of any commentators of even their own creed, the Arabs here convocated thinkers from all parts of the then small world. From France under intolerant bigotry of Philip and Louis *le Gros*, from Germany under the fourth and fifth Henry, from Rome under the overbearing Pope Pascal II., and from Venice under the more lenient Doge Foledro,—from all Christian Europe, in fact, as well as from Persia and Egypt, the philosophers of every shade of opinion were permitted an audience. What a splendid period ! and what a crowning contrast with the ignoble intolerance of Christian autocrats were these splendid thinkers, the high-minded followers of the prophet !

THE JEWISH SCHOLARS

And now, glancing superficially at the Jewish representations in science contemporary with these noble reliquaries, we find that the generous befriending of the persecuted Jews, who suffered under Christian rulers, by the Moslem Califs, brought to the benefactors' religion many a staunch adherent of the Tadmud. Among the important converts who own Cordova as their native city, is the celebrated Rabbi, Moses Ben Maimon, or more generally known, Maimonides, the forerunner of the great Hebrew phil-

osopher of Amsterdam, Spinoza. His learning was gigantic. Like a sponge, that daring intellect absorbed everything within the reach of his times. Commentaries on the
scriptures, on medicine compiled from Egyptian, Greek, and
Hindoo sources, treatises on astronomy, and reconciliations
of the Old Testament with reason—everything unattempted
and worthy for the present exigency he absorbed and
poured out again, refined by the sunlight of his own fierce
intellect. Avicebron, of Malaga, although before Maimonides in point of time, was the author of the celebrated
" *Fons vitæ*," that work of profound pantheism, wherein
is taken that perilous stand in maintaining the universality
of the opposition of Matter and Form throughout the sensible, the intelligible, and the moral words, arguing at the
same time their indissoluble unity. His influence was felt
by Maimonides, while likewise, in spite of unbounded enthusiasm in the doctrines of Aristotle, refused to admit " the
eternity of the world *ex parte ante*," and that divine intelligence alone contains the possibility to universal forms.

But it is not necessary to dilate to a fuller length this
list of learned Moslems and Jews ; it but remains to say
that the splendid schools of Seville, Cordova and Salerno
were turning out doctors of medicine, jurisprudence and the
kindred sciences by the score and that soon the whole of
the benighted, corrupted, relic-worshipping world outside
the Moslem dominions were flooded with Jewish exponents
of the several perfected and modernized sciences, and it became necessary for the church to surpress them by not suffering the Christian world to employ their services, under
penalty of death to both employer and scholar.

The educational standard during the period of Saracenic
ascendency and at its meridian in Spain, was commensurate
with the highest standards of the contemporary achieve-

ments of the East. Ali, the fourth successor of the great
prophet, left injunctions with regard to the education of
youth, which was as faithfully regarded here as at the
hearthstone of his chief. Nearly a hundred public libraries
were sustained at different points—an astonishing mark of
the times—and every mosque had a school for the education of youth in the simple rudiments, and in the pre-
cepts of the Koran. The Mahommedan maxim " that true
wisdom in a man is mor to be regarded than any religious
or other conviction he may entertain," was generously
carried into practice. With such a country such a language
with a possibility in its breadth and bounty to give to human
thought the keenest and nicest gradations of word-coloring
with a religion which enthused the devoted even to fanaticism, yet enlarged their hearts and found them manly in
their liberality, with politeness and personal grace the
chief factor of Cordovian social life, and such masters of
the arts and sciences to give weight and quality to the education to the youth how could it do otherwise than evolve
a civilization at once unique, in comparatively foreign soil,
exalted by reason of the dignity of its purpose, and refined
by the very nature of its climate, and wealth, and national
character?

And yet all this has passed away. The school where the
portly gownsmen paced the brilliant porticoes, the fireside
where the story-teller from Babdad and Morocco gathered
the household and told and retold the stories that gladdened
the hearts of their forefathers, the pulpit, the rostrum,—
everything that edified the race and proved its superiority,
has passed away ; but the spirit lives and has a being in the
achievements of our own times, and certainly a place in the
heart of him who contemplates these relics with a genuine
sincerity of heart.

www.ingramcontent.com/pod-product-compliance
Lightning Source LLC
Chambersburg PA
CBHW020338030726
47496CB00007B/1930